AFTER MATH

MAYO THOMPSON

AFTER MATH

ART, MYSTERY—PART II

DRAG CITY | CHICAGO

DC846

No resemblance to situations or persons
living or dead is unintentional.

Drag City Web Address:
www.dragcity.com

Printed in the United States of America
Library of Congress Control Number: 2021941482
ISBN: 978-1-937112-36-3

First Edition

On est là, qui mal y pense.

—Gruyère

1

Jasmine was excited—her suit for ownership of the Pollaiuolo was finally coming to court.

Though he was happy for her of course, Leo's feelings about the statuette remained unchanged. When his grandfather presented him with a photograph of the promised object on the occasion of his twelfth birthday, his embarrassment became family legend. He hoped it didn't get to be evidence.

Things were somewhat simpler. His grandfather having died in prison the year before, with him, his counter-suit, Jasmine was now sole litigant v Albania. The family were sanguine. Were the general still alive at least one of them would have had to testify under oath to the facts of the matter anyway.

It would of course be awful going to court. A few asked Leo what Jasmine wanted? Was it money? Leo explained money didn't come into it. She had ideas.

Jasmine was a smart cookie. How she had bounced back after the Venice debacle was impressive, splitting with Dr. Harmoni without acrimony and persuading him to trade her his interest in their gallery for her interest in their condo and a selection of works from their collection. How she had organized their meeting and setting the deal for the statuette in motion had been intoxicating. The night they closed they met in the Rogner bar for what both had come to fear, without knowing the other felt the same, would be their last drink.

It hadn't even been close.

"So, Ms. Tajismini—"

"So, Mr. Skanderj-Pollo—"

"It has been an honor and a pleasure doing business with you."

"Thank you. I feel the same ways about doing business with you—honored, and pleased."

They toasted.

"You know, you always said you want to show it, and I never dared ask—but—will you?"

"I'll show it."

"How do you expect it will be received? Is that a dumb question?"

"Not at all. I imagine the response will be sensational. There'll be a real spectacle."

"Invite me, please."

"Of course."

"May I ask you something—personal?"

"Go ahead."

"Does the—work affect you?"

"I don't want to give you any wrong ideas about me but I think it's pretty hot."

"I asked!"

"I get jazzed by erotic art generally."

"Wow."

"It has always been like that with me."

"Really?"

"Really. You not?"

"I like jazz but I have my frontiers. That photograph I gave you with the bill of sale? To be honest, I couldn't look at it."

"Erotica is not everyone's cup of tea. But—I can go for things."

She laughed.

"What's funny?"

"I just remembered going for something—one time —when I was a student. Ever taken to a museum when you were a student?"

"A time or two, but no statue or painting I ever saw had erotic effect on me."

"This was Pompeii—on a summer field trip. Ever been there? No? It's uncanny. There's the city, but it's empty. I was with a group of students and our Art History professor? And—we had a guide. We saw everything—the amphitheater, villas, everything. What got me going were the frescoes in the brothel—love-making illustrated—"

"Um-hmm."

"—And a statue of a household god whose Latin name I can't recall. The Greeks called him 'Priapus'—god of phallic functions."

"Ah."

"There are lots of examples. Figures vary. The only convention is a disproportionately large, anatomically correct, private part."

He smiled.

Perhaps it was then that she felt that she might be able to cast her fate to the winds with him.

"It was outside, locked in a wooden box up on stilts. Our guide was pure theatre—taking out his keys, looking for the right one, finding and inserting it, twisting it, opening the lock and removing it, putting it on top of the box, swinging open the door carefully and slowly standing aside with a small, knowing smile. Our collective gasp made him happy. The figure looked like a dwarf. Whatever he was, he was dwarfed. Our eyes popped. He let us look for awhile before beginning his lecture, in a flat voice telling us what it was made of, how, when, its symbolic significance, protocols involved in its ritual use, in Greece, differences in Rome, etc., etc. My head was swimming—his droning on, the statue, the images from the brothel—and it was hot. When he finished he smiled in a weirdly friendly way and looked us over, making eye contact, here, there, with a boy, a girl, this one, that one—happily, never me! It was creepy. All at once, like a bad man at the playground with a bag of candy—in a voice that was innocence itself—he invited anyone who might care to to touch it—feel how remarkably cool the metal was, even on such a day?"

Her eyes grew sleepy, heavily lidded. She smiled faintly.

"I—felt a—sort of—primal urge."

"Uh-oh."

"I stepped forward. Our professor gasped."

Leo laughed.

"I—looked at it—and—"

"And!?!"

"Our guide looked at me—"

"And!?!"

"I smiled at him—and ran my fingers—just the tips—along his fantasy."

Leo's Adam's apple bounced.

"There was a big 'oooooo' from everyone."

"What did he do?"

"Fell over backwards, almost."

She imitated him—eyes wide, mouth agape.

Leo's laughter was sweet. It made her laugh. They laughed together. Without thinking, she reached and ran her fingers through his hair, looking at him tenderly, seeing the embarrassed boy.

He melted.

The happy couple's cottage was in the family compound in the countryside outside Tirana, a veritable fortress situated on a bluff. His rooms were in the west wing, hers in the south. The arrangement suited them well. Most mornings they breakfasted separately but lunched together, schedules permitting, and dined together in the evening as often as possible. They had their fun too of course from time to time in both suites.

Jasmine adored fresh flowers. There was always a big arrangement in the gallery, and three at home—one in Leo's rooms, one in hers, the last in the library.

She thrived on going to the Central Market. It was fun—arriving before dawn, the sights, the sounds, the smells. She loved stopping for a coffee in the Red Poppy Café after.

Sipping her *espresso* one morning something less than a month from her court date, out of the corner of her eye she saw Tile talking and laughing with her old friend, Bari B.

Of all people talking to of all people.

She felt positively ill.

Back home she hurried to Leo's door and knocked softly.

"Lofti?"

He was still in his dressing gown, reading.

"Dearest?"

"Sweetheart, please—I'm—do you mind?"

"Whatever is the matter? Please come in."

He put down his book and rose to greet her, took her hands and kissed them. They were ice cold. She appeared truly worried.

"What is it, my love?"

"I saw someone."

"Someone? Who?"

"I never imagined. The last person I hoped ever to see again, especially now."

"That football player?"

"Kiss me."

"Darling—"

"I was in the Red Poppy—you know how I like to drop in there—after buying flowers—for an *espresso*. And—and there he was."

"Heavens—did you speak to him?"

"No—he may not even know I saw him. I don't think he did. I hope he didn't. I acted as if I hadn't seen him. Oh, Lofti—it's so awful."

"Darling."

"Now I can't go to the market anymore. Or the Red Poppy."

"You can."

"What if he's there?"

"Oh, my darling."

"What if he talked to me?"

He stroked her cheek.

"I like fresh flowers. You know how I do. I like getting them. Especially in winter. I like to have a coffee before coming home. And—oo, why now?"

He touched her nose.

"Don't worry."

"He's trouble. I feel it."

She held him tight.

"I love flowers! I need flowers! And—and now I can't go anymore. Oo."

"Calm, dearest. Send Fatima."

Jasmine sniffed.

There was an idea.

"Oh, Lofti—do you think?"

"Absolutely."

"To see if he's there. If he isn't, maybe it was just a coincidence, see it's safe to go back? Oh, Lofti."

2

Two nights earlier at the Chrome Exchange—

Tile had to give up working days altogether. The odd looks, the jokes, behind-hand and in-your-face insults looked like never leaving off. Nights there was no risk of collegial mockery, and being busy generally meant no time to think about the Pollaiuolo Affair. He had yet to do his after math properly and was feeling increasingly bad about it, especially now, with news that Jasmine's claim was going to court.

"Evening, Mr. Tile."

The security man appeared, a husky twenty-something.

"'Evening, Tedi. Everything all right?"

"All quiet, Mr. Tile."

"Are we alone?"

"You're the only agent—my partner is downstairs."

The lad leaned in the jamb.

"Ask you something, Mr. Tile?"

"Shoot."

"What happens here in the daytime?"

"Day trading."

"Is it hustle, bustle? People yelling, signaling. Like you see in movies."

"Not anymore."

"Oh."

"A lot is run by algorithms. You interested in business?"

"Not really. I like science. I'm studying Biology."

"Like it?"

"It's interesting—there are facts. I like it a lot—Mr. Tile? Ask you? You used to be a footballer, right?"

"Once upon a time."

"I heard. Goalkeeper."

"Checking up on me?"

"People talk about you."

"What do people say?"

"That you were very good, great, a champion."

"We were champions. What else do they say?"

"You have a bad temper."

"Had, Tedi—had."

"Ask you something else?"

"Sure."

"Did you really jump in a canal in Venice, Italy, chasing after some kind of porno art?"

"That's true. Wow. Look at the time."

"It's eleven."

"Pardon?"

"Eleven."

"What time is it?"

"Eleven."

"Please?"

"Eleven o one now."

"When o one?"

"It's… What are you doing, Mr. Tile?"

"Waiting for an elevator that will never come, Tedi."

"A what?"

"To take a trip nowhere that begins somewhere."

"Okay, okay, I best be on my way anyway—Mr. Tile?"

"Tedi?"

"Thanks, Mr. Tile."

"For what?"

"For talking."

"Thank you, Tedi, thank you. See you tomorrow night."

"I'm off."

"Have a pleasant weekend then. See you next week!"

Tile liked the kid.

He was thirsty and needed to think, which as usual made him think of Naj. He was still too embarrassed to try explaining anything to Naj. It was pathetic.

He gathered his coat and hat and hit the street trying to decide where to go besides home to rerun stray thoughts of canals and porno art and what bloody not until overtaken by sleep.

Being downtown, he reviewed prospects. The piano bar at the Xheko Imperial was nice but there was lounge music, and thoughts of Pablon. The Rogner bar could be full of Americans. The International was out; chrome brokers drank there at all hours. The pool bar at the Plaza would be full of kids, some in bathing suits, even at that hour, in that season!

So it went until he remembered Winnetou's, an already ancient bar he drank in when first he came to town.

He hailed a taxi.

Winnetou's was behind a heavy door down an alley in the old part of town, not a million miles from Naj's. He pulled it open, wiped his feet, took off his hat and pushed through the slit in the thick felt curtain surround and smiled. Inside, it was cosy, and virtually unchanged—Winnetou still hung over the bar—and there was no music.

Without looking, he took off his gloves and checked the few customers—two men at the bar, three playing Skat at a table in a corner, a couple lost in each other in one booth, and, a booth back—his guts yawned—the little cop Jasmine sent to warn him off, waving and beckoning.

Unable to think what else he could do, Tile went.

"Well, well, well. Mr. Tile. Good evening."

"Officer Barisha."

He laughed.

"Just Barisha, please—join me? Please—I'll explain."

He was older, a bit heavier, but still in green. The mullet was gone. So was the attitude. Now he was all friendly like, and his hair was a red shock on top, back and sides clipped down to stubble.

Tile shrugged, hung his hat on the rack, took off his greatcoat and hung it up, slid into the booth.

The little man beamed.

"I thought you were strictly a Naj man."

The barmaid came.

If she remembered him, it didn't show.

"Good evening."

"Good evening."

"What will you have?"

"Gin, please. Gordon's."

"Gordon's—how? Neat? Rocks? Tonic? Juice?"

"Rocks. A double, please. You have Texsun pink grapefruit?"

She smiled darkly, nodded and went. Perhaps she did remember him.

"Got your mind on your money? Or—"

"Pardon?"

"—Or your money on your mind?"

"My what on my what?"

"Never mind."

They looked each other over.

"You said something about explaining?"

"Indeed. Sorry. I'm not a cop."

"What? Anymore? You quit?"

"I never was one. I was playing one."

"Playing one?"

"I'm an actor—primarily."

"Seriously?"

"Primarily."

Tile looked at him blankly—what the fuck.

Barisha wrinkled his brow, narrowed his eyes and squinted at him.

"Hm—funny—you're not angry."

"Funny?"

"'Funny' maybe isn't the word. Don't get me wrong—you don't seem to care?—and I'm glad."

Tile shrugged.

"How'd you get the part?"

"Jasmine and I come from the same place. She thought you were a stalker."

Tile's gin and juice arrived.

"Thank you."

"You want to start a tab?"

"Please."

Barisha had a glass of tea, a plate of gray bread and onions in front of him, and a still frosty glass of vodka. He raised it.

"Cheers."

"Cheers. Ask you something?"

"Shoot."

"Jasmine—?"

"What about her?"

"I understood her sending cops—you guys—both times—but, when I persisted? What did she say when she called you off?"

"We cancelled. After our second visit we told her you weren't afraid of cops and that taking it to the next level wasn't on. All we had were those fake IDs. We couldn't haul you downtown, show you guns, Allah knew what. She made a face and asked for your card back. We gave it to her. She read it and tore it up. We laughed."

"She has little bitty pretty feet for such a big woman."

"I'll drink to that."

"And funny shoes. Interesting—she read it? Both sides? You remember? 'Pollaiuolo'? Written on the back?"

"We saw that. I had no idea who that was. Sali did—being an artist."

"Did she?"

"I don't know?"

"You didn't wonder?"

"I didn't ask. Sali either. We took the situation for what she said it was—a man thing."

"I was chasing the statuette."

"I'd like to see that statuette."

"I'd like not to."

"You've seen it?"

"I've seen a photograph."

"Really?"

"It comes to mind, willy-nilly."

Barisha's eyes became slits. He grinned.

"Describe it, hmm? Please?"

"Men having sex."

"Okay—how?"

He dipped a bit of bread in his vodka, popped it in his mouth, all ears.

Tile looked him in the eyes.

"There's a ruined column, and steps. One stands at the top, a slender fellow, legs spread, propping himself on the column. At the bottom stands the other guy, big, one hand on the slender one's hips, one on a shoulder. He's halfway in. The poses work. It's realistic. Their expressions are lifelike. It's elegant."

"Man. Phew—how big is it?"

Tile laughed.

"What's funny?"

"Nothing—just made me think of someone else asking me that—forty-five centimeters high maybe. Pollaiuolo's *Hercules and Antaeus* is—which I imagine represented gold-standard in small bronzes at the time."

"You think it's by him?"

"I don't know. I'd say it's in his style at least?"

"Ah, the visual arts. It's delicious how taboos can be worked in that field for fun, and profit."

Tile laughed. They both laughed.

"Where's your partner?"

"Sali emigrated. He has relatives in Sicily, outside Palermo."

"Sounds nice."

"The food certainly."

"He's an artist?"

"He's a painter."

"What school?"

"He says he's a Formalist. His stuff doesn't look so formal to me."

"Painting just is formal."

"You actually are interested in art."

"When I said so—on the occasion of your first visit—perhaps you'll recall?—you pointed out that I shuffle papers for chrome brokers."

"Playing 'bad cop.'"

"So you don't actually think that being in chrome export and having an interest in art are necessarily mutually exclusive?"

"I see I was right thinking that would get your attention. Sorry. Seems it still does."

"It does, rather."

"I do not think that it is impossible."

They studied one another.

"Too bad you're not an artist—you could paint the statuette."

"Ha."

"I wish it would come out."

"How? Why? What for? Where could you show it?"

"Peep show?"

"Are you interested in art?"

"I look."

"What at?"

"Contemporary."

"'Of this time'—is that a real category?"

"What do you mean 'real category'?"

"What's the difference between 'Contemporary Modern Art' and 'Contemporary Art'?"

"I'll have to get back to you on that."

They drank for a bit in silence.

Tile broke it.

"I wouldn't mind seeing Jasmine."

"Haven't seen her since she married."

"Saw that on the news. How was the wedding?"

"Wasn't invited."

"No?"

"Her husband belongs to a circle of squares where proles such as I are not welcome."

"Where are proles such as you welcome?"

"Oh, here and there."

"I like it here."

"By the way—Texsun pink grapefruit juice?"

"I used to come here."

"What brings you back?"

"I wanted to be alone."

"Oh well—that's something like me. I like this place in part because nobody I know does."

"I like it in part because there's no music."

"Why not Naj's? The music?"

"More, much more than that—I'd get offered Bellinis."

"You no like?"

"I like *prosecco* well enough? I no like people getting cute."

"What can you do?"

"What can you do?"

It was getting chummy.

"Chrome interesting?"

"It's a business."

"You like business?"

"I like it all right."

"Until I read your card I didn't even know there was chrome in Albania."

"Chrome is a treasured natural resource. Its mining and export are vital to the national interest."

"You should do voice-over. What's the deal? With chrome?"

"You want to make stainless steel? You need chrome. And—"

The barmaid came.

"Need anything, fellows?"

They looked at their glasses, each other, nodded to her practically in unison, broke out laughing.

"And—something for you—chrome is one of the elements that makes emeralds green."

Tile made sparkle eyes. Barisha laughed.

"I see stainless steel sculpture."

"Where do you see that?"

"Contemporary fine art magazines—online. By the way, thanks. Try as I might I was never able to conjure a satisfying image of anything you could make an esthetically pleasing statuette out of. Your description has been a big help."

"You're welcome."

"I guess I'm interested in art—but feel mostly indifferent to what I see. I pay attention more to the social implications of consumer taste and choice."

"To what?"

"I bet you could sell chrome statuettes of two guys fucking."

Fresh drinks arrived.

"Cheers—oh, my goodness. Where have my manners been? Would you care for some bread and onion?"

"No, no thanks. Cheers."

"Ask you something? You understand women?"

"Understand women?"

"Dames? Right? Were one with whom you thought you shared something approaching natural affinity, and for whose project you felt something you at least thought of as solidarity to inform you that they believe in love and hate, have reasons for doing so, and can explain, but won't because you wouldn't understand, your being Albanian, their being Kosovar, what would you think?"

"I'd think she's being funny. That happen to you?"

"Sung. Hearing that—after what happened earlier, it felt cruel, deliberately—humiliating."

"What happened earlier?"

"Never mind."

Tile laughed.

"You sweet on the dame?"

"'Sweet'? Now there's an antique term. No. Nor was I sour. I wanted to trip with her. You 'sweet' on Jasmine?"

"I lusted for her."

Barisha laughed.

Tile signaled the barmaid.

"What can I get you?"

"Another, please."

"I too, will have another, thank you—and tea? Please? Thanks."

"What does 'mostly indifferent' mean?"

"Huhn?"

"Awhile ago you said you're 'mostly indifferent' to art people make? Mostly—but not completely?"

"I said that?"

"And something about paying attention to consumer choices?"

"I've no idea what I was trying to say."

He shrugged, looked at Tile innocently.

"You don't recall saying that you are indifferent—largely—to what people make but not indifferent—to—?"

Their drinks came.

"Thank you—to what people make of it? Socially, culturally? Something like that? To change the world?"

"No?"

Tile laughed.

"Where did your 'bad cop' come from?"

"The heart. I method act."

"You were convincing."

"Thank you. Generous of you, and nice to hear. Sali and I felt we had to be. We knew who you are, your reputation."

Tile blushed.

"You're known to be dangerous. I lived it like that. I was totally wired. Sali—"

"I'm not dangerous."

"I was scared—which suited how I wanted to play. 'Officer Sali'?—okay, not him. His air of calm confidence, relaxed, even laconic authority? That's no act. He's the kind of fellow who isn't afraid of anything or -one? Not even you? A natural yourself—you saw that, and trusted him. I was happy to see that. He actually is the really nice fellow I think you thought you saw."

"You seem nice enough."

"I can be."

Barisha smiled.

Tile responded in kind.

"Allah be praised."

"Why do you think Jasmine asked you guys to see me off instead of going to the real cops right off?"

"Hm? I don't know? Habit? Culture? Dr. Harmoni? I don't know. It never occurred to me to ask. Where we come from, folks don't always run to the law right away. Back home, she'd have had her brothers call on you."

"I wonder if she ever did tell Dr. Harmoni?"

"No idea."

Barisha chased the last of his vodka with bread, took a bite of onion, poured fresh tea.

"Where'd you get started with this Slavic thing? You're only missing caviar."

"Ah—if only. Is there caviar anymore? I picked it up in Russia. There you get black bread, also a pickle with your onion if you want it, and, depending on where you are, schmaltz if you want it. I was tour managing and emceeing for an Austrian techno band, two guys from Tyrol. Don't ask how I got the gig. We played Moscow, Petersburg, Kiev, Tblisi."

"Funny, how that all fell apart in the end."

"Not fun funny."

"No, not fun funny. Does your jacket come from Russia with love?"

"No. It's from Skipfilm. I had a bit part in a dog they were making about discos, dancing and drugging—a period piece. I spotted it in Wardrobe. It's my second skin."

"Were you a dancer or a druggie?"

"Both, of course."

"What was the film?"

"*One Step Forward, Two Steps Back.*"

DIZ
MUZ
WUZ
ZANGI CAN
DJ C-CRAIN
15.2.20
TIRANASAURUS TEX
HYRJA FALAS

3

The following night—

Finding no parts since ages, among other things, Barisha still worked for Tiranasaurus Tex managing the stage and emceeing gigs weekends.

To the stage and sound crew he was "the green man," "Mr. Sympa" to the bar staff, waiters and waitresses, and it seemed, somehow special to Tex. Certain he was capable of stabbing you in the neck with a biro if provoked, to Security he was "Joe Pesci."

The night's bill comprised Dizmuzwuz, a Technometal outfit, headlining, Zangi Can opening, and the house DJ. The Zangi's press kit advertised them as "trading in Kurdish folksong, played in the style of James Brown, at the speed of sound." What Technometal was was self evident.

Ever since fouling up introducing The Skipit Club and being humiliated for it on stage, Barisha took pains to find out what bands' names were, properly speaking.

"Any special way Zangi Can like to be introduced?"

Nothing.

"Right. Cool. The nosh and drink okay?"

Nothing.

"Right. Cool. We wish you a great show. If you need anything, Gjerjh—the hulk by the stage door—will help you. You're on at ten-thirty for an hour. If the audience want an encore? One tune. If they go nuts—?"

Nothing.

"—We'll see about a contract."

Nothing.

"Just kidding."

Nothing.

"Right. So—seriously—where was I—uhm—ah, right—Gjerjh will give you a heads up at ten. Ten minutes later, he'll appear with his trusty flashlight so nobody trips and gets hurt—"

Nothing.

"We keep it dark backstage."

Nothing.

"For a 'thank you' he'll say, 'break a leg.'"

Nothing.

"Break a leg."

Dizmuzwuz's drummer, an associate professor of Geology at the University, did the talking.

Bari smiled at her, nodded to her fellows.

"How do you wish to be introduced?"

"We're just Dizmuzwuz."

"Okay—just Dizmuzwuz."

"No 'just'—Dizmuzwuz."

"Got it. Dizmuzwuz. Does Dizmuzwuz have a meaning?"

"It's the proper name of our band."

"That's it?"

"What do you mean?"

"I understand that it's the proper name of your band but—it sounds like it's short or long for something —does it relate to something? A fantasy world?"

She looked at her bandmates, back at him.

"We're—"

"Wait wait!—Don't tell me. It just hit me—is it made up of parts of your three names?"

She smiled.

"I am Diz—Dizeña. He is Muz—Mustafa. He is Wuz."

"What Wuz? Wuz what?"

"Just Wuz."

"Okay. Wuz is Wuz. All right. Got it."

"One last thing—we're on at midnight..."

"Right."

"Call us ten minutes to showtime. From eleven until then? We want to be alone."

"You want to be alone from when?"

"From eleven to ten minutes before we're on."

"From—sorry?"

"From eleven?"

"What floor, please?"

She smiled.

He grinned impish-schoolboy.

"Break a leg."

On his way to his office, Gjerjh appeared.

"What's up, dude?"

"They asked for goofballs. They want goofballs."

"Who do?"

"The what's their names—the Zingo Kings."

"What did you say?"

"What are goofballs."

"Thanks. I'll see to it."

As he told them what was what they stared at the floor.

He shrugged and went back to work.

An hour later, the room went silent and he took the stage.

> "Good evening, ladies—and, good evening, gentlemen —ready to dance?"

There was cheering.

> "Leading the way in sway—tonight?—roots representatives from the parliament of funk—l's and g's, g's and b's—Zangi Can."

They boogied and were funny—there would be Kurds in Turkey's way forever.

Their crowd was enthusiastic, mostly girls, cheering and clapping hard for an encore to no avail. Zangi Can would not return.

Dizmuzwuz needed no introduction.

> "Ladies? Gentlemen? Dizmuzwuzzzzzzzzzz..."

They were intense and got two encores.

Security breathed a collective sigh of relief when the evening ended without incident, the Zangi's audience being predominantly dancers, Dizmuzwuz's mainly trancers and chancers. The atmosphere had been weirdly wired.

Cashing out receipts, Tex whistled a happy tune. The door was good; the bands were good; the kitchen and bars scored.

Barisha called by his office on his way out.

"What you whistling, Boss?"

"'The Yellow Rose of Texas'—*I dream of Rosalie but The Yellow Rose of Texas is the only one for me.*"

"Ha—cool. All right, then. Well—right, then—g'night."

"G'night, Bari. Good show tonight."

"Thanks, Boss."

"You're welcome. Thank you."

"See you next weekend."

"Bari, hang on—got a minute?"

"What's up?"

"Like a toddy before you head out?"

"That'd be nice, thanks."

They went down to the main bar and sat on stools.

"I like the openers."

"They were good."

"I think they've got a future."

"You talk to them?"

"I did. I told them I liked their stuff."

Barisha smiled.

"And Dizmuzwuz?"

"They cook."

"Boss—no wonder you're a legend."

Tex smiled.

"Am I?"

He was a former tough guy who'd made his way wrestling on television, playing the hometown predator on EuroSat. Having come along the hard way, he liked the idea of giving locals a leg up.

The homophone came to him in a dream. "Tex" came from living for a year with his great-aunt and her husband in Baytown, Texas, US of A. Not only the nickname followed him home. There was a story too, about a fight in a bar with a fireman. It was said to have lasted forty-five minutes, only coming to an end when they crashed through a screen door and wound up in a ditch by the parking lot where Tex was alleged to have bitten off one of the man's ears. True or not, it linked him forever in lore to the likes of Mike Tyson, Luis Alberto Suárez Diaz, and Count Dracula.

The story served him well, in and out of the ring. He wisely left why to rumor. Folks might speculate, but none dared ask, or test him.

"Any chance your staying on?"

"I'm not going anywhere."

Tex looked hard at him.

"It's just a mood, Boss—winter discontent—somehow to be made glorious—preferably before summer."

"All right, Bari boy—all right. Cheers."

"Cheers—hey, guess who I bumped into yesterday night?"

"I give up."

"'The Beast of Bern'."

"Perly?"

"You know him like that?"

"I do. We came to town around the same time. He's a funny fellow. He used to come in here late. Where'd y'all meet?"

"Winnetou's."

"Whoa, Winnetou's. Man, that brings back memories. You go there?"

"Sometimes."

"Hell, that's where we met. I was tending bar."

"Wow. Word. You knew him before Bern then?"

"He got shafted. I've seen the video. The striker was acting—no offense. Perly never deliberately kicked him. Oh, he may have given him a bit of a blow in the gut accidentally. They were both going for a high ball at the edge of the box. It was even—you remember that trouble Perly got in in Venice?"

"A bit."

"The ref in Bern? He was the same guy that hired Perly a couple of years ago to find that pornographic statuette?"

"Oh, fuck—right."

"How's that for irony?"

"Life can be strange—so what happened? They say Mr. Tile went crazy."

"He did. He went mad. He chased the guy all over. They had to restrain him. It took some doing. There was a big scandal. It was in all the papers. Wouldn't happen these days, not with VAR, slo-mo, three-hundred-sixty-degree swing shots. Back then it was strictly plain vanilla. For my money, a free-kick would have been more fair—give Perly a yellow maybe, to keep the game under manners? Red? Red was sadistic."

Barisha shook his head, downed his vodka.

"Rotten luck. He seems—okay."

"For sure. But with Perly—I don't know. Things—find him."

They looked at each other, smiled.

"Getting late, Boss."

"It is."

"Thanks for the lowdown, and for the drink—thank you—for this time, thank you—really—g'night."

"'Nighty-night, Bari boy. Go easy."

"I will. You too."

It was too late for Winnetou's, too early for bed.

Instead of home, as he did occasionally, he went to the Central Market, bought the early edition of *Panorama Sport* and settled with a pot of tea at a corner table in the Red Poppy to people watch.

The place was busy—steamy and loud, clashing plates and voices, bustling porters and vendors, early market customers and night owls, scraping chairs, sometimes, theater people. He was happy not to see any.

Dizeña came to mind.

He tasted her name. Thanks to Tile he had a chrome-plated conversation opener.

He was working on his first line when two shapes appeared.

"Dude?"

"Oh, hello chaps."

It was the Zangi's rhythm section.

"What's up? Have fun tonight?"

"We've got a bone to pick with you."

"Really?"

"You weren't fair."

"Not fair?"

"No, dude. You said, if we needed anything, we should ask that guy by the stage door."

"Yeah. You said he'd help us."

"He wasn't any help. You neither."

"Yeah."

"Gosh. What did I say again?"

"You said 'if you need anything, ask that guy for help.'"

"And you thought 'anything' meant 'anything whatsoever.'"

"Come on, dude. You run a cool gig and you said, 'if—you—need.'"

"What we 'needed' was not just 'anything whatso—fucking—ever,' it was something essential, dude."

"To being in a proper state to deliver our proper goods, the real dealio, dude. We specified our need."

"It wasn't right."

"We weren't us."

"Your set went well. Perhaps because you weren't yourselves."

Tile loomed up.

"Good morning, Officer Barisha, g'morning, gentlemen."

The Zangi boys traded "Officer Barisha!?!" looks.

Barisha smiled broadly.

"Ah, Mr. Tile. We meet again."

Tile peeled off his gloves, looking the two up and down.

They looked nervous.

"Am I interrupting?"

"These fellows are in Zangi Can—a band. They played Tiranasaurus Tex's place last night. Bass—drums."

Tile smiled politely.

They nodded.

"So—right, fellows. Anyway. Thanks for stopping by. I heard you. Good show. Thanks again."

"Yeah—uhm—okay—right. Let's go."

"Right—sorry—aren't you Perlat Tile?"

"I am."

"Man o man—my dad's a big fan."

"Thanks. My best to him."

"Dude, take their picture. So he can show his dad."

They looked at Barisha, at Tile.

Tile shrugged, smiled.

Bass got out his 'phone.

Drums lined up adjacent, stuck out his tongue as far as he could and made a "K" with his fingers.

Tile put his arm around the kid and smiled.

Snap.

They shook hands.

"My respects to your father."

"Thanks."

The two sloped off talking fast to each other.

"Strong kid, shoulders like a wrestler. What you reading that rag for?"

"I'm a football fan. And— "

He held it up and looked at Tile over the top edge.

"You could have been a real cop."

Barisha laughed.

"We meet again."

"I'm not reverse-stalking you. Nor front-following."

He laughed again.

Tile laughed.

"You work for Tex?"

"Weekends."

"What's those boys' music like?"

"Fast funky folk."

"Funky folk?"

"Kurdish folk songs played funky and fast."

"They Kurdish?"

"Sympathizers."

"You political?"

"Not really. You?"

"Never."

"Whoa!?!"

Barisha rubbed his eyes.

"'Whoa!?!' what?"

"I thought for a second I saw Jasmine!"

"Where?"

"Over there—by the *espresso* machine. The other night? We talked about her too much—I'm having visions."

4

The following weekend—

"Fatima?—Fatima!"

"Coming, Your Majesty."

Her voice echoed from the cellar.

"What are you up to?"

She arrived, grinning broadly, eyelids heavy, stinking of *kif.*

"What can I do for you, Highness?"

"'Highness' yourself. Don't grin like that. You look like a gargoyle."

"What's a gargoyle?"

"Never mind. I want to talk to you about something."

Fatima laughed.

"Something? You mean the future."

"Come upstairs."

Jasmine looked anxious in a way Fatima had not seen before but knew must be something to do with her worries about that improper statue.

She suggested Jasmine pray.

Jasmine wondered, to what?

Not to what—to whom—to Allah.

But Jasmine did not believe.

It did not matter—Allah knew her, everything about her.

What she wanted?

Of course.

Allah knew she wanted the statuette?

Of course.

Then he also must know that she did not believe and was, moreover, not about to get down on her knees and pray for his help taking legal possession of something that was already rightfully hers.

Fatima nodded and rocked.

"Allah also knows whether you're going to get it or not."

"Are you trying to frighten me?"

"You frighten yourself."

"Stop it. Listen. I want—excuse me—I would like for you to go to the market tomorrow and buy the flowers for next week, please."

"You're not feeling well?"

She took Jasmine's hand and saw a shadow.

Instead of to Sicily, driven on east by storms and currents, the bark Fatima'd drifted away from Libya on in hope ran aground in Albanian waters, on the coast near Durres.

Albanians knew sailing away. Perhaps it was that, and, to some extent, perhaps paradoxically, depending on how you looked at it, a residual too of a sense of international solidarity ingrained in them as a people with peoples of non-aligned third-world countries that contributed to Fatima's and thirty others' being treated humanely. Whatever it was, she thanked and praised Allah.

Circumstance took her to Tirana. There she found work at a flower stall in the Central Market, one favored by Jasmine Skanderj-Pollo, born Tajismini, wife of Leo Skanderj-Pollo. Her ability to see and say sooth impressed Jasmine, and both enjoyed what each felt was a special understanding. Soon Fatima became Jasmine's maid. There was even a mild resemblance. Fatima could have been Jasmine's smaller, darker cousin.

"Let me fix your hair—there... Don't mess with it!"

"I look like you."

"You should be so lucky. Once you have the flowers —you know what I like—go to the Red Poppy. Be there by five, latest. Stand at the bar. Order an *espresso*."

"I prefer a *cortado*."

"They don't have it."

"I know. As I used to, I'll order an *Americano*."

"Whatever! Stand on the left, at the end of the bar, so you can see the room. Face like this. Good. Notice who's sitting to your left—without turning your head—look—look, like this."

"You show me how to look out of the corner of my eye, sister? Words fail you?"

"Fatima! Listen. See who sits to your left. If you see—"

"A large man?"

"Yes—you saw that? Well—good. Fine. If you see a large man, don't look at him. And don't make faces—"

"Gargoyle faces?"

"Not any faces. See if he notices you? See how he reacts."

"Don't look at him, don't make faces, see if he thinks I am you."

"Exactly. I doubt he'll approach you. If he does—just be yourself."

"If he's handsome?"

"You're not looking for a boyfriend."

"I wouldn't mind. I like big men."

"Fatima!!!"

"And if he's not there?"

"You can praise Allah. I'll just say, thanks."

At the Red Poppy, as luck would have it, sure enough, a hulk she felt must be the large man in Jasmine's hand was sitting at a table to her left, back to her, with someone she could see only in flashes—a small man, in green, talking animatedly.

Had Fatima been able to hear she would have heard Barisha joking with Tile about how often they seemed to be running into one another these days, and about the statuette.

Tile had no energy for any of it. His head was swimming from crunching numbers and filling out forms late into the night for what had been days but seemed like weeks.

He was about to excuse himself when Barisha's look stopped him—the look he had had when he thought he'd seen Jasmine.

Tile resisted turning around.

The moment passed.

Before Barisha could start in on the statuette again, Tile seized the opportunity to stand and wish him a good morning with apologies.

He was sorry. He felt a wreck.

They looked forward to meeting again. At Winnetou's perhaps? Tomorrow? Perhaps—wherever. Indeed—the way things were going it seemed inevitable they would see one another somewhere, probably soon.

For a laugh, Tile reached and gave Barisha a card. Barisha read it and tore it up.

They both laughed.

> "He was there—tall—two meters *au moins*. His back was to me so I dared look. He was sitting with a man I could only see bits of until he sagged for a moment. In that moment I saw a small man, with red hair up like that, dressed in green. I had to think of Colonel Gaddafi. Our eyes met. He saw me as you. I looked away. When I was able to steal a glance again—in the corner of my eye—the big man was standing, gathering his things. The small man stayed sitting, looking up at him. They spoke for a few moments. Then, the big man got something from his coat and gave it to the small one—maybe a card. He looked at it, tore it up. They both laughed. The big man walked past me on his way out. He took a look, up and down. I can't say he didn't think of you. In the corner of my eye the man in green was watching the big one go. And he looked at me again. Had I looked at him I'd have had to blush—as if he were my husband. I paid and went outside. There I saw the big one get into a taxi. Here is the number."

5

Leo doubted Tile was up to anything even if he was there. Still, he felt he had better look into it quietly since in fact he did happen to be.

What a mess.

Fatima's noting the taxi number was interesting for what it suggested about valuable intelligence in Libya, and about her, having such wits about her.

He rang Naj.

"Lofti?"

"Naj—"

"Something up?"

"I'm afraid it's your friend, Tile."

"Afraid? I'm listening."

"What is he doing appearing to Jasmine just now?"

Leo recounted the sightings at the Red Poppy.

"I don't take that for 'appearing.' He's probably just sitting there. The exchange is just around the corner. Tax time is coming. He works nights."

"He was with someone Jasmine knows."

"Who."

"His name is Barisha, an actor. He's from the village she's from."

"Coincidence would be my guess."

"That's what I think! Jasmine's claim?—will they call him?"

"Without doubt but so what?"

"What do you mean?"

"He has the liabilities. Listen, really, Lofti—don't worry."

"Will they call me?"

"I doubt it. What would be the point? Their argument is that Jasmine's claim is without merit because you sold her something you never had actual possession of. They don't need to call you to show that."

"Jasmine says her lawyers will argue that the piece never belonged to the old state. I don't know how that can be proved. They're having trouble finding records."

"Take heart. Say what you will about the old days, records were kept. If your beloved paternal grandfather stored his archive at the Marxist-Leninist Institute for safe keeping it will have been memorialized somewhere by somebody. He was a comrade."

"Can something like that be admitted into evidence? Old state stuff?"

"Of course."

"What should I tell Jasmine about Tile? She seems truly anxious about him."

"Is she? Don't tell her anything. That's her fight—none of your business, unless or until she wants it to be. Don't worry. She's tough. If you feel you have to tell her something, tell her something loving, like, tell her not to worry."

"I do."

"That's the spirit. Keep it up."

6

Ring ring.

"Jasmine?"

"Bari."

"Nice you ring, dear. I just spent the day wondering what that dog and pony show at the Red Poppy was all about? First, you, then, what? A body double?"

Jasmine laughed.

"That's my Fatima."

"Your Fatima?"

"My hand maiden."

"How delightful."

"From Libya."

"How delightful."

"A seer."

"From your tone of voice I'd say you'd like to have a sorceress."

She laughed.

"What are you up to?"

"Whatever do you mean?"

"Come come—it's B."

Jasmine sighed.

"I want the statuette—that's what I'm up to. What are YOU up to?"

"I?"

"What's up with you and what's his name?"

"Strange. We bump into one another lately."

"I don't believe in coincidence."

"Do you believe in anything?"

"I believe in you."

"Sweet."

"And trust you to speak the truth."

"Still?"

"It goes without saying."

"So, why are you saying it?"

"Smarty—for something to go without being said it has to be said. Has he said anything about the statuette?"

"That he wishes he could stop seeing it."

"What?"

"In his mind's eye."

She went silent, crunching for a moment.

"You don't think he's still after it."

"No."

"Or that he wants me not to have it."

"If you think that, you're tripping."

Maybe she was.

He told her how they'd met at Winnetou's, of all places. He'd thought the guy was strictly a Naj man.

Looking later at the photograph Leo had given her as a promissory note—the way Tile had described the poses was mad but he was right about Hercules looking about halfway in.

She rang Cyn.

She was on edge.

Why?

She'd been called to testify.

When.

That afternoon. She been served with a summons that afternoon.

Jasmine's blood raced. She smiled. Good.

Good? Bloody hell. This was all she needed. Was she going to have to answer questions about fucking Tile?

Jasmine didn't know.

That would be just great. Dr. Ali was already going nuts. Bloody hell.

She could finally write her memoirs.

She might as well. After fucking all.

"Should I talk to him?"

"I don't know. Do you want to?"

"He's bound to be called too, I guess."

"Probably."

"Do you think they'll ask him about our fucking?"

"I don't know. My lawyers won't ask him—nor you."

7

Ring ring.

"Goodness—is that you?"

"What's up, big boy?"

Booty's in the eye of the beholder.

He tingled.

"Up? You know me."

Her laugh was low and slow.

"Been awhile."

"Uh—yeah. Day-job. You know."

"Mm-hmm. Word is you only work nights these days."

"Luckily not tonight— "

He listened to her breath.

"—Makes things simple—simpler. Still mad at me, baby?

"Grrr—just furious."

"Hmm. Sorry."

"What are you up to?"

"Reading."

"What?"

"Philosophy. Holism."

She laughed.

"Want company?"

Dangle tingle, the invitation followed.

An hour later she knocked.

When he opened the door, she poked a finger in his tummy button.

"Buzz."

That laugh.

He kissed her on both cheeks.

She smelled good.

He gave her a shot of Gordon's, neat.

"Warm you up."

"You know—you—."

"I'm happy to see you"

They looked into each other's eyes.

She was there and somewhere else.

"Let's kiss."

He kissed her.

She let him.

"Here, let me help you."

He had her down to a cute Mickey Mouse t-shirt and matching knickers before she put a hand on his chest, touched his cheek.

"Perly—"

"What is it, my little skateboard princess?"

"Wait."

"How long? Baby?—How long?"

She sat up.

"I've been summoned."

"Summoned?"

"To appear."

"For Jasmine's thing?"

"Yes. Have you?"

"No—at least not yet."

"What do they want?"

"I don't know."

"If they expect me to say anything against Jasmine—oh, fucking hell. Perly—Perly—Perly."

"Cyn, Cyn, Cyn."

They held each other until she broke off, drank some gin, looked at her watch.

"You going?"

"I'd better."

"Where's your car? I'll walk you."

She dressed.

He walked her.

"New car. Nice. Fast?"

"Fast enough. I'm sorry, Perly."

"Don't be. It's nice to see you. Come again."

He took her hands.

"Ring again. Come again. Anytime."

He smiled.

She smiled.

"Bye-bye, big boy."

"Bye-bye, honey. Safe home."

He liked Cyn coming round, and felt sad when she left.

The hall lights went out on him short of his flat. He cursed and felt his way along, rejoiced upon reaching his door and sliding his key into the lock—a small triumph—something he thought to himself he needed just then.

What in the fuck was going on with that no-fuck fuck visit?

He turned on BigTime 7, made a sandwich, and got a shock when the late weather came on. There was Barisha, shorn, shaven, brown suit, white shirt, florescent paisley tie, pointing to a coming storm.

Next morning Tile rang him.

"Officer Barisha? Did I see you on TV last night?"

"Don't 'Officer' me anymore, okay?"

"Sorry?"

"Recall calling me that at the Poppy? The other morning? When I was talking to those musicians? That's why I'm in weather now."

"You're in weather because I greeted you as 'Officer Barisha'?"

"Yes."

"What's that got to do with those boys?"

"Thanks to those 'boys,' as you persist in calling them, every musician in Tirana now thinks I'm a cop."

"Good grief."

"I've had to quit Tex's."

"That's terrible."

"It is in a way. Luckily I was tired anyway."

"Man, I am sorry. What if I talk to them?"

"Talk to Zangi Can?"

"Explain."

"Assuming you could get in touch—out of curiosity—what would you say, pray?"

"Don't be sarcastic. Let's see—easy—give me a minute."

"Take your time."

"Let's see—I could say, 'Boys—.'"

"You haven't been listening. 'Boys' is something only certain people in music get to call musicians."

"Men?"

"They aren't soldiers."

"Guys?"

"You're not a waiter."

"Fellows?—nice meeting you fellows—uh, the other morning?"

"Do go on."

"Uhm... let's see—when we met—wait—wait—Must be fun—you guys?—you fellows!—being musicians, playing places, meeting people. How's your father? I know Tex. Must have been a kick—working with that

Barisha. What an actor! Man o man. When we met, I thought he was a cop! Can you believe it? Ever see *One Step Forward, Two Steps Back*? Wild—mind you, Mister B, I can't find it anywhere."

"Dude, touching—really—you tell the story of our first meeting, then that? A disco dancing druggie in the 'eighties was—probably still is today—at the very least an informant."

"Tex? Could he set things straight?"

"I'd have to explain too much and that wouldn't work either. Anyway. It's too late. Let it go."

"Sorry. Really sorry."

"Never mind. I'm a BigTime 7 TV weatherman now. 'Chilly today, hot tamale'—that's a Tex joke. Guess what else? I actually did hear from Jasmine."

"Oh?"

Tile's blood raced.

"What did she have to say for herself?"

"She's such a character. She's tripping about the statuette, says, when she wins? She'll show it. If I don't make it in weather, maybe she'll give me a job. There's money in art."

Tile felt bad.

"Listen, Bari—good luck—either way. Did she say anything about me?"

"Nah—you called to testify?"

"No."

"No?"

"Uhn-uh. Not yet, anyway."

8

State's witnesses included Mrs. Sojia Y—sister of the late Ahmet X; the head janitor, chief carpenter, and two secretaries from the National Museum; a guard from the National Archive; the night doorman, and the head concierge from the Xheko Imperial Hotel; Mrs. Cynthia Faqu; and Mr. Perlat Tile.

Jasmine's sole witness was Leo's mother's brother, Uncle Timo—ancient partisan, comrade and friend of Secretary Hoxha and his lady wife, patriarch of what remained of the Skanderjs—like the Pollos, an heroic, patriotic family.

In their opening, State promised the court would hear of two plans to acquire the contested property, a Renaissance statuette attributed to the Florentine master, Antonio Pollaiuolo. Although its subject matter was of a forbidden nature, in the matter of ownership a principle was at stake—nothing less than the legal status of property that had belonged to the old state in the new. The first plan was the devise of Mr. Pablo Pablon and his accomplices, Dr. Giorgio Giorgio, and Mr. Tiki Vari. It had been a success. The second plan followed from the first—they might even say it had been necessitated by it. That plan involved the plaintiff, Mrs. Jasmine Skanderj-Pollo, née Tajismini, her friend, Mrs. Cynthia Faqu, and Mr. Perlat Tile. Their plan had been a signal failure. The people were in court because Mrs. Skanderj-Pollo hoped to acquire by legal means what she and her fellows had failed to acquire by devious ones. The court would be called upon to decide the merits of her claim with in mind what brought them there that day, and what it said about her. She acted as if what happened in Venice stayed in Venice. She was wrong. It counted in Tirana. With that, they called their first witness, Mrs. Sojia Y. Was it true that she had sold her late brother's ashes to Mr. Pablon? Yes. Had Mr. Pablon said what he wanted them for? No. And she hadn't asked? No. Hadn't she been concerned at all what he had in mind? He'd said her brother's ashes would be in a famous cemetery surrounded by artists and composers. Did he say where this heaven was? In Italy—she was happy—Ahmet loved music. Really? Yes, and Italian food. Really? It was a blessing—the family was poor—Mr. Pablon had come with a nice box—he was very polite, nice, very respectful—he'd complimented them on the urn... He took care putting it in the box... She felt—it was like she was at the funeral her brother deserved the family couldn't afford... He seemed truly sorry—for Ahmet—for them... He brought a bottle of wine, and flowers. Touching—had he been alone? No, there was a fellow with him who translated and closed up the box—they were poor... It was a blessing. How had she met Mr. Pablon? A janitor at the museum was a friend of Ahmet's, and the family's—he introduced him. And how had she felt, later, when she got the ashes back? Confused at first, and, to be honest, disappointed for Ahmet. When was that? From what she could remember from the news, two days before she heard what happened in Venice. That would be June fifth? Yes—she thought so—a messenger had come with the urn. In its box? No—a carrier bag. The public laughed. The chief justice scowled and rapped. And, out of curiosity, what had she done with the ashes since? The urn was on a table in the sitting room. Jasmine's lawyers had no questions. The witness was excused.

State called the head janitor at the National Museum. Yes, he had introduced Pablon and Mrs. Y. How had that come about? Dr. Giorgio… A moment, please—for the record—was he referring to Dr. Giorgio Giorgio? Yes. Chief curator at the National? No—*senior* curator. Fine, senior curator—please go on. Dr. Giorgio asked if he knew someone at the City Crematorium—he needed some human ashes. Human ashes?—What had he thought of that? Thought?—He hadn't thought anything. Really? What was he supposed to think? It hadn't struck him as odd in any way? No—Dr. Giorgio sometimes asked for special things. When? For an exhibition sometimes. An exhibition of human ashes? He shrugged—Dr. Giorgio was an art expert—maybe he'd asked him because he was an ash expert. There was laughter. The chief justice rapped and cautioned the witness not to make light of such a serious matter. The janitor apologized. And did he know anyone at the City Crematorium? No. So—how had he made the connection with Mrs. Y? Purest good luck—if that was the right way of looking at it—Ahmet was an old friend—he knew he'd just died, knew the family, knew they had no money for a funeral, not even for cremation—as far as he was concerned, Dr. Giorgio's wish was providential, a gift from Allah—he'd made the deal for both sides, a sum in advance to pay for cremation and an urn, the rest upon delivery of the ashes. That had been quick thinking. He was glad to have been able to help both sides. Did he have any idea who the man with Pablon had been?—The one who boxed up the urn? No. How much had everything cost Pablon—all in? Three-thousand US dollars, in cash. Jasmine's lawyers asked, had he been compensated? He had—ten percent. The witness was excused.

The museum's carpenter testified to having been instructed by Mr. Vari. Just a moment, Mr. Vari?—the assistant curator? No—he wasn't "the" but "an" assistant curator—in the Renaissance department. Fine—and what were his instructions? To build two crates. Two? Yes. Had the assistant curator said what they were for? No—he'd given him the dimensions, even specified what wood they were to be made of—he'd gotten on with it. Did he recall the dimensions? He could do better than that, producing the memo from Mr. Vari with the dimensions and material specifications in the assistant curator's own hand. He also provided his working drawings. State asked that both be entered in evidence. Jasmine's lawyers looked over the memo and drawings. They had no objection, or questions.

The museum secretaries appeared in the afternoon session. They provided unassailable detailed evidence of Dr. Giorgio's and Mr. Vari's meetings with Pablon in the form of their respective schedules—logs, of dates, times and places—and records of their telephone calls, incoming and outgoing, all entered in evidence without objection or question.

With that, the first day came to an end.

The first witness the next day was the guard from the National Archive. He testified to having let Mr. Tile in because he was who he was after all. This was the night of the sixth? It was. Was that entirely proper—letting him visit after hours? He didn't know—he'd done it. Had Mr. Tile been alone? He had. What had happened? Pardon? What did he say?—What did he want? To see General Pollo's lots. And he had shown them to him? He had. Just like that? The general was a football fan—he supported Mr. Tile's club. Did he in fact? He'd seen the general at games—often—and he was in the news again at the time—he guessed Mr. Tile was curious. Had he been present when Mr. Tile found that the box containing the statuette was missing? He had. How had Mr. Tile reacted? He'd seemed a bit puzzled at first. What had he said? He didn't say anything. Did he do anything? He counted the boxes. Counted the boxes? Yes, then counted them again—and... And what? He made a face. There was a sprinkling of laughter. The chief justice tapped. A face? Yes. What kind of face? Kind? Yes—did he look—what?—angry?—disappointed? He didn't know—a mix of all of that. Was that when he himself learned a box was missing? It was—he reported it the next day. On cross, Jasmine's lawyers returned to his saying that Mr. Tile had been alone—no women had been with him? No—he hadn't seen any. That was all, thank you. On redirect, State asked, what if the box Mr. Tile was looking for had still been there?—Would he have tried to stop Mr. Tile had Mr. Tile wanted to take it away?—or helped? The guard looked helplessly at the justices.

How did they expect him to answer something like that? State withdrew the question—they were just musing. He was excused.

State called the Xheko Imperial doorman, an old partisan. He bowed cordially to the justices. Yes, he was the night doorman. How did he know Mr. Pablon? He didn't know him. He knew that he was an hotel guest? Yes. Did he see him often? Every night he was on duty until he checked out—he saw him when he came out, looking for a taxi, or on his way somewhere or returning on foot. Did he come and go a lot? He was in and out. Had he ever chatted with Mr. Pablon? He begged State's pardon—chatted? Had they ever spoken? They might say "good evening" to one another or "good night," him, "thank you" for holding the door, getting him a taxi. Nothing more? That was all. Any idea where he went? No. Was he always alone? Mostly, though he had seen him with one fellow, sometimes another, sometimes both of them. Did he know who the two were? No. Had he ever heard them talking? No. Did he know Mr. Tile? Not personally. But he knew who he was? Of course—everybody knew who he was—he was a great footballer. How often did he visit? Some—he couldn't recall exactly how many times. Had he always come alone? Yes—except for the last time—that night, he was with two ladies. Did he see the two ladies in the courtroom? The doorman pointed to Jasmine and Cyn. He didn't know their names. State asked that the record show that the witness had pointed to the plaintiff and Mrs. Ali Faqu. So ordered. What had they wanted? He guessed they were looking for Mr. Pablon.

What had happened? He'd held open the door for them. Then, what happened? They went in. Yes, yes—then what? In a while, they came out and rushed to the car the lady with silver hair gave the valet—it was a snappy job, so he left it right in front—they got in and sped off. State wondered, had he been on duty when Mr. Pablon checked out? Yes—earlier the same night. Had he been alone? Yes—he was the only doorman at that time of night. No, that wasn't what they meant—was Mr. Pablon alone? Oh—no—the two men?—the ones he mentioned earlier?—they were with him. How much baggage did he have? Two suitcases, a briefcase and two boxes. Two boxes? Yes—both made of wood. Heavy? Not very—both about the same. How big? So-by-so-by-so, both of them. On cross, Jasmine's lawyers wondered, was Mr. Pablon a good tipper? The old boy reported he had never been tipped.

The Xheko Imperial concierge testified that he recognized Mr. Tile immediately, the very first time he came to visit Mr. Pablon. So, he was a football fan? He was. When was the first time Mr. Tile called on Mr. Pablon? Two days after Mr. Pablon checked in. How often had Mr. Tile visited? Sometimes daily. Had he always come alone? Always except for the night of the sixth—that night there were two women with him. Were those women in the courtroom? Yes, those two, sitting at the back. State asked again that the record show that the witness was referring to the plaintiff and Mrs. Faqu. So ordered. And what did they want? They were looking for Mr. Pablon. And what had he said? He had been reluctant to give out information on a guest. But he had had he not? Yes. To save plaintiff's attorneys the trouble—had Mr. Tile given him a tip? Yes. And he had accepted? Reluctantly—not to be rude. So as not to be rude themselves, they wouldn't ask how much. The public laughed. The chief justice rapped. They'd heard from the night doorman that when Mr. Pablon left there'd been two men with him—did he know who they were? No—they were frequent visitors but he'd no idea who they were. How often did they visit? Every day, sometimes more than once. Ever with Mr. Tile? Not as far as he knew. On cross, Jasmine's lawyers had but one question—had either lady said anything? Not a word. State had one more thing—the doorman testified that Mr. Pablon's luggage included two boxes. Did he know anything about that? Yes. Mr. Pablon had asked that they be kept for him in Left Luggage. For how long had they stored them? For four days prior to his checking out. Thus ended the morning session.

In the afternoon, having set the stage for Venice, State called Mrs. Cynthia Faqu. They wondered how she and Mr. Tile met? She met him one night after a show at Tiranasaurus Tex's club. They were at the show? No—he had come over. He came over? Yes—to where she lived, she and her husband. Dr. Ali Faqu? Yes—her husband invited him when they met at Naj's. At Naj's disco? Yes. Wait—she was at Tiranasaurus Tex? Yes. And her husband was at Naj's disco? Yes—he had been at the show at Tiranasaurus Tex's but he left and went to Naj's. And there he met Mr. Tile? Yes. So Mr. Tile was never at Tirannasaurus Tex's? That's what she said—she left Tex's after the gig and went home—when she got there, there was a party going on.

And Mr. Tile was already there? Yes. Who else was there? Her husband, a friend of his, and two women she didn't know. No one else? She couldn't remember there being anybody. Had she and Mr. Tile talked? Yes. Did they talk about art? Some. About Pollaiuolo? No. Was Ms. Tajismini, as was, mentioned? No. So—he had no idea that she and Ms. Tajismini were friends? As far as she knew—no. And she had no idea that he was trying to find the statuette? No—well—not exactly—not the statuette, not then. Pardon? She'd known Tile was after a Pollaiuolo for a while. Oh?—Since when had she known? Since the night he visited Jasmine—Ms. Tajismini—at her building—Ms. Tajismini had come to visit her afterwards at the Art Academy and told her what had happened. So, she, so to say, knew who Mr. Tile was, and that he was looking for a Pollaiuolo practically from the beginning? She thought so. That night, at the party—had she and Mr. Tile gone to bed together? Jasmine's lawyers objected—how was that relevant? State argued the nature of Mrs. Faqu's relationship with Mr. Tile was pertinent to understanding events leading up to Venice, and what had gone on there. Overruled. So—had they slept together? Cyn looked down. The chief justice told her she must answer the question. Yes. That night? Yes. Any other time? Jasmine's lawyers asked were State keeping score?—or what?—What were they trying to suggest? State weren't trying to suggest anything—they merely wondered about Mrs. Faqu's motivations. She was instructed to answer the question. Yes. More than once? A few times. A few?—Wasn't it several times?—Wasn't that why she had gotten involved?—Gone to Venice? She still didn't know why really. How had it come about? She had given Mr. Tile a lift to Pablon's hotel. A lift? He had telephoned wanting help. Did he say what for? Not over the 'phone. So, she picked him up? Yes. Where? At a café, Where? Downtown. Near the National Archive? Pardon? Had she been alone? No—she and Ms. Tajismini'd been having drinks when Mr. Tile rang. And Ms. Tajismini decided to tag along? Yes. Perhaps she was thinking Mr. Tile was getting closer to the statuette she so coveted? Jasmine's lawyers objected on two counts—State's characterization was argumentative—and, really, how was Mrs. Faqu expected to know what Ms. Tajismini was thinking. Sustained. What had Mr. Tile said when he saw she wasn't alone? Hello. There was laughing. The chief justice glared. Where did he want to go? To the Xheko. Did he say why? He wanted to see Pablon. Did he say what about? The statuette. So the three of them had gone to Pablon's hotel, found out that he had checked out, and was on his way to Venice with the prize. Was that a question? Yes. Yes. What had they said to one another when they learned Pablon and Co. had skipped town? Said?—She couldn't recall exactly what they said. Was it something like, "we've got to get that statuette"? Objection. Sustained. Whatever it was—they'd decided on pursuing Pablon to Venice hadn't they? She guessed. And in Venice, they plotted—how was it? How was what? Was there complete trust among the three of them? Trust? Agreement? Agreement? Were she, Ms. Tajismini and Mr. Tile of one mind? Pardon? Were they all on the same page? It had all been a bit crazy—like a dream.

How crazy?—Had she and Mr. Tile slept together? Objection. Overruled. No. What happened on the big day? They'd hired a skiff. A skiff? Yes—a small boat—with an outboard motor—she and Ms. Tajismini were waiting in it. Where? In a side-water off the canal leading to the Grand Canal for Mr. Tile—he was supposed to join them when Pablon left the church—then, they'd follow. And what happened? He arrived soaking wet. What had she thought? At first—that it was funny. And Ms. Tajismini? She thought it was funny too. What did he say? That he had slipped and fallen in the canal running to meet them. And after that? They understood that it was over—the funeral boat was gone. Indeed—the funeral boat was gone—and with it the statuette. How had she and Ms. Tajismini felt?—Were they disappointed? She couldn't speak for Ms. Tajismini—she hadn't known what to think—she just knew everything had gone wrong. Indeed, and how—how did things stand after? Stand?—After? Between them—after everything went wrong?—Were she and Mr. Tile still... friendly? Objection. Sustained. What about she and Mrs. Skanderj-Pollo?—Were they still friends? Really, wondered Jasmine's lawyers aloud, what had that to do with anything? State said they just wondered—thieves often fell out. Jasmine's lawyers protested. State withdrew the question. On cross, Jasmine's lawyers asked what the three of them had hoped to do with the statuette, had they succeeded in taking possession? They never discussed it. Had she and Ms. Tajismini at least planned on doing the right thing? Right thing? Returning it to its rightful owner? State objected—facts not in evidence, and Jasmine's lawyers were leading the witness. Sustained on both. On redirect State asked, did Ms. Tajismini ever sleep with Mr. Tile? Cyn was dumbstruck. Jasmine's lawyers shouted objection—incompetent and immaterial. State shouted the people had a right to know just how entwined these people were. They were overruled. The chief justice admonished both parties to keep it civil, and adjourned court for the day.

The next morning, State called Tile. When was the first time he'd met Pablon? Nineteen-eighty-seven. Where? Bern, Switzerland. What had been the occasion? A football match. Pablon had been the referee? Yes. And Mr. Tile a player? Yes. In goal? Yes. In fact, he was team captain that match, wasn't he? Yes. And over a controversial call Pablon had shown him the red card. Yes. His team lost. Yes. Flashing forward to Twenty-eighteen, Pablon contacted him? Yes. For what? To hire him. For what? He didn't see why he had to go over all that again. Please answer the question. Did he have to? He was so ordered. To find a statuette Pablon said was by Antonio Pollaiuolo. Hadn't he found it a bit odd—the referee who sent him off coming to him for such a thing? It was funny—but he'd said he was an art and antique dealer—he was looking for an export agent—that was the angle that made it make sense. Made it make sense? Yes—once it was found he said he wanted to export it—and wanted him because that was his specialty. Indeed—and, with his help at every step, Pablon did precisely what he said he wanted to do—he exported something he stole from the National Archive. Jasmine's lawyers objected—facts not in evidence. Sustained. What had Mr. Tile thought upon seeing Pablon again? Funny how he didn't care anymore. Really? He hadn't been the least bit agitated? He wasn't angry anymore. Angry!?!—Wasn't that putting it a bit mildly?—He'd been in a blind rage—there'd been an international scandal over his behavior when Pablon threw him out of the game hadn't there?—and there Pablon was, in his office, offering him—what? A job. A strange job to say the least, wasn't it? What was strange about it?—It was a job—a job's a job. Really?—had he ever heard of the artist? No. Pablon had shown him a photograph of the piece had he not?—with its explicit subject matter? He had. Any idea where he got it? No. Had that been what decided him on jumping in? There was loud laughter. The chief justice hammered. What had it looked like? What had what looked like?—the statuette? They would come to that—no, the photograph—how was it?—was it a new photograph, a recent print? He didn't know enough about photography to say when it was from—it didn't look new. Could it have been from as long ago as The Great Patriotic War? He couldn't say—he'd never seen an actual photograph from back then—he was born in the 'sixties. Had he been shocked? By what? The subject matter obviously. He shrugged—like he said, he was born in the 'sixties. There was light laughter. The chief justice hammered and demanded order. Tile was asked to describe the piece. He told them pretty much what he'd told Barisha, minus characterizing the figures' expressions, or mentioning that he found the piece elegant. State let his words hang in the air for a moment. What happened next? When? After Pablon showed him the photograph. He'd gone to Gallery Harmoni. Why there? Pablon sent him—he had one of their cards. He had the gallery's card?—Then Pablon must have been there himself? Tile shrugged. He hadn't thought about it—people pick up things like that at hotels. He hadn't wondered at least why Pablon wanted him to go instead of going himself? He'd asked him that. What did he say? He'd said it would affect the price if they knew he was interested. So Gallery Harmoni were in possession of the statuette? He seemed to think so. And what had happened when he went? Happened?—Nothing happened, more or less. What did he mean, "nothing... more or less"? The lady of the house wouldn't see him. He was referring to Ms. Tajismini, now Mrs. Skanderj-Pollo? Who else? What had he done? Reported to Pablon. And what did he say? That he should try again. Had he? Yes—he had gone to her residence to try again. When? If he remembered rightly, the night of the same day. Was he able to talk to her then? Yes. Had they talked about the statuette? Not exactly. How was that? He'd brought Pollaiuolo up. What had she said? She'd called him a jerk and told him to fuck off, more or less. The public roared. The chief justice hammered. Tile apologized but excused himself—that's what she had said—more or less—he'd been asked. The chief justice understood but admonished him not to use such language. If such an occasion arose again, he should use a euphemism. Tile promised he would. State turned to the export documents he had filed on Pablon's behalf for the remains of Ahmet X. What had been the dimensions of the box? He consulted his papers and was asked to read them out.

He read them. How had he known them? Pablon gave them to him. Did he ever meet any of Ahmet X's loved ones? No. Did he ever see the urn? No. Its box? No. Had it been in the archive or later that he put two and two together? Pardon? Perhaps one and one was more appropriate—the question was when had he figured out that the size of the box for the urn was just right for the statuette? When he saw that its box was missing. How had he felt when he saw that? Felt? Was he angry?—disappointed?—shocked?—did he feel foolish? He'd had mixed feelings. The public tittered. The chief justice glared and tapped with his pencil. What had taken him to the archive in the first place? He'd had a 'phone tip. From whom? He didn't know—a voice he didn't recognize. And he'd believed it? Why not?—by then he'd tried pretty much everywhere else he could think of. When he saw that the box was missing, did he think he'd been double-crossed? Double-crossed? Hadn't he been engaged by Pablon to find the statuette? He had. So, they were in it together? Not together in the way they were suggesting. Then, what had he thought? That he was a bit behind the game. There was a sprinkle of laughter. The chief justice threatened to clear the court. And so, with the then Ms. Tajismini, now Mrs. Skanderj-Pollo, and her friend, Mrs. Faqu, the three of them had chased Pablon to Venice where Plan Two was formed—to steal the statuette from the man who had stolen it from the archive. That wasn't right. What wasn't right?—Pablon hadn't stolen it from the archive? No, it wasn't right that they intended to steal it from Pablon. If not steal it, what did they call what they were trying to do—liberate it? They were just trying to get it. And what were they going to do with it, once they "just got it"? A long silence. They hadn't gotten that far. Jasmine's lawyers had only two questions: had he at any time thought Ms. Tajismini as she then was was involved in any way with Pablon? No. And Mrs. Faqu? Her neither. He was excused. Jasmine's lawyers reserved the right to recall him? State had no objection. It being a Friday, proceedings were recessed early for the weekend.

Tile's lawyer congratulated him. For what? Maybe he wouldn't be prosecuted for having entered the archive with intent to steal. In her opinion, State were setting the pick for an offer of immunity.

9

Beginning of March, Coronavirus hit town. All parties were informed that Mrs. Skanderj-Pollo v Albania would proceed on Zoom as soon as arrangements could be made.

Both sides agreed to proceedings being streamed.

BigTime 7 News got rights. They'd been covering the story on tape and playing highlights. Barisha had been making goings-on part of the weather report since day one. People liked him. He was moved from the nightshift to midday, then primetime to work in tandem with a female colleague, a real meteorologist, stage-name, Dr. Dani Nova, known as "Super Nova" around the station for her very shapely proportions. She and he clicked with each other and the public, working the report like a trial, her playing expert witness, him cross-examining her on pressure fronts, their backsides, cloud banks, fog banks, precipitation, adding spicy bits, trading on new-at-the-job charm, and making a meal of his near-complete ignorance of meteorology outside experience of the effects it accounted for.

When lockdown came, masks and distancing made playing hard. Eventually, they were compelled to isolate and join the broadcast from their respective homes.

Thinking Zoom penetrable, Jasmine and her lawyers met in a secured video interface. They warned her that State's aim to portray her as party to a conspiracy with Mrs. Faqu and Tile to steal the statuette was real—the pick was set with that business about Tile discovering at the archive that he had been beaten to the statuette. How was she implicated in that? She had gone along with him after that happened, knowing he was after the statuette, and being known to be after it too—to want it, no matter what. Were they serious?—She went to Italy to rescue the statuette from a thief. Technically, she couldn't be charged in Albania for anything that happened in Italy but State might try to conjure something within their jurisdiction. How? They'd gone to Pablon's hotel—it could be asked if they had been ready to take the statuette by force?—It was hard not to infer from Tile's visiting the archive that he at least was no longer interested in finding the piece so he could give it to Pablon. Could something like that work? It would be a stretch but State might try. Why? To force her to settle perhaps?—If they could make anything along those lines stick they'd be in position to offer to drop any charges in exchange for dropping the claim. And Tile? State had cross-examined their own witness—they hadn't objected because the worse he looked, the better for her, no matter what—their worships had let it go because he wasn't on trial—yet—Tile was helpless—toast—there was nothing for it—were State able to get traction with their intent-to-steal hypothesis they'd offer him immunity, make her out to have had plans of her own, and surely try to drive a wedge between her and Mrs. Faqu, offering her immunity as well. Okay—did they anticipate her being charged? They couldn't say—State's case for a conspiracy among them was as weak as their effort to retrieve the statuette actually had been—State's real case rested on ownership by default—the new state inheriting the property of the old—on that score, were they able to find the records of General Pollo's arrangement with the Marxist-Leninist Institute that they were looking for the game might be hers—they had someone working on it. She was glad to hear that—she nor Mrs. Faqu ever had any intention of stealing anything—they were trying to recover the work—she couldn't vouch for Tile's interest—whatever it was, she wanted the statuette in order to return it to its rightful owner so as to do proper business with him to acquire it—Tile's jumping the gun spoiled it—wasn't that enough to show he had plans of his own?—And wasn't her doing business with the very man who owned the work, buying it, and marrying him, proof of her good faith?—Those were facts they should put in evidence.

10

Uncle Timo appeared from his study. He was greeted and handled with great respect. To Jasmine's lawyers he confirmed that his nephew owned the statuette. On cross, State pronounced themselves not anxious to go into any great detail but had to ask, it was their duty to ask, how had the late general acquired the statuette? The old man said nothing for a long moment, then told the world that the general—as a young officer, after the protectorate collapsed, at the end of The Great Patriotic War—liberated the statuette from a Nazi. So, it was war booty? He didn't know that that was the right word for it—Command had looked into where the Nazi had gotten it—thinking that it surely was not his to begin with—in the end no-one came forward to claim it. And the general was allowed to keep it? Allowed—yes—Command allowed him to keep the statuette. How could he claim ownership? Uncle Timo chuckled. He found the question humorous? Humorous?—no—laughable—Command gave it to him—war is war. Really—and how could he say so definitively that his nephew owned it? He had been present when the general gave it to young Leo—it was a birthday gift. For some reason Jasmine and her lawyers couldn't unpack but were glad of, not least because of Leo, State made no mention of the photograph. Their guess was that State didn't know about it, and probably hadn't been able to establish where Pablon acquired the photograph he had. Court recessed for the day. Commentators spoke of the old man's great dignity in an awkward situation.

At the next session Jasmine's lawyers recalled Tile. He was at home. They found it intriguing, his experience of Venice—there he was, with Mrs. Faqu and Ms. Tajismini, trying to figure out how to get the statuette?—Was that fair to say? It took a minute for Tile to think before replying—yes. How had he thought that would go? What did they mean? In the drink? Pardon?—no. When he, Ms. Tajismini and Mrs. Faqu arrived, what had they done first? Checked the burial schedule. Where? City Hall. Who's idea had that been? Ms. Jasmine's—sorry—Ms. Tajismini's. And, having learned when and where Pablon and Co. were going to carry out the charade of a funeral for Ahmet X, what had they done next? They'd found an hotel and ate dinner. Had they discussed what to do? Yes. And come up with a plan? Yes. What was their plan? Same as Mrs. Faqu said. They'd like to hear his understanding. Why? Because, the way things had gone, it seemed to them at least that perhaps somebody somehow misunderstood something? Well—Ms. Tajismini and Mrs. Faqu were to wait in a small side-water near the church while he watched. Watched? The church where they were holding the funeral service. What church was that again? Santa Maria dei Miracoli. So—to review—the plan was that Ms. Tajismini and Mrs. Faqu should wait—? Right—in the boat they'd hired. While he watched the church? Yes. And then? When the cortège was aboard and the funeral boat was underway, he was to join them. Then what? Together they would follow the hearse to the cemetery, hide and wait until the funeral party left, take the statuette and return to Tirana. But he had jumped the gun? He guessed they could put it like that. They let that sink in. How did that happen? Pardon? They had a plan—he jumped the gun—they had to wonder—whose plan had it been? What did they mean? Was it Ms. Tajismini's plan?—or his?—or Mrs. Faqu's?—whose? They'd all contributed. Parts? Yes. Which parts were his?—which theirs? He couldn't remember every detail. Why not take them in order?—the boat—the side-water—his watching the church—his running to meet them—the idea of their following the funeral boat to the cemetery—watching and waiting—then seizing the day?—So—the boat—whose idea was that? That was Ms. Tajismini's. The side-water? All three of them. Watching the church and running to meet them? His he guessed—what did all of this matter? Please—following—watching and waiting—seizing the statuette?—those were all also his ideas—right? He hesitated. Yes—he guessed. In fact, Ms. Tajismini and Mrs. Faqu only thought what kind of boat, and where to wait, hadn't they? Tile shrugged. What changed his mind? Pardon? Why had he decided not to follow the plan? After a long silence Tile said he still didn't know. Hadn't he planned that too?—Pulling the plug on the greater plan? What? Wasn't his jumping into—trying to jump into the funeral boat about cutting the chase out? What? He wanted the statuette for himself, didn't he—without having to share it with Ms. Tajismini, or anybody else, didn't he? That was crazy. Was it?—Come—he'd played Ms. Tajismini and Mrs. Faqu—knowing full well when he laid it out that his idea of following the funeral boat and somehow getting the statuette after Pablon & Co. left was nonsense? How was that!?! They guessed Ms. Tajismini and Mrs. Faqu hadn't quite thought it through—at the cemetery the urn would have to be removed from the box to be placed among the greats of art and music—everyone would see that, instead of an urn, there was a statuette in the box—Pablon's game would be up. Tile was silent for a moment. He hadn't thought of that at the time—he knew that now. Oh, really?—They were expected to believe that? Hadn't everything worked out for the best?—in the end? What did he mean "for the best"? The Italians grabbed Pablon and the box—the statuette was back in Albania, and he had learned something. And what, pray tell, was that? That he needed to get a grip on his impulse control issues. Had they been in court, there would have been laughter. State had nothing on redirect.

Hearings adjourned for the weekend.

Jasmine and Leo had been watching in the library. Fatima brought in tea. Afterward, Leo excused himself and repaired to his suite to think. Her lawyers had done a decent job of impugning Tile's motives at least but, if they asked him, State had made enough of Jasmine, her old friend, Mrs. Faqu, and the dread football player conspiring in the first instance to take the statuette from Pablon somehow to be trouble. Also, Uncle

Timo's testimony hadn't seemed likely to be the last word on ownership, what with all that about war booty.

He rang Naj.

Two days later, Jasmine's lawyers called Naj. He was at his desk, behind him, his wall-full of photographs of noteworthy friends and celebrities. Jasmine's lawyers thanked him.

His pleasure. He hoped to be of help to the inquiry.

Terrible, the virus.

Horrific.

Indeed. They wondered, had he been following the case?

He had. He accused the solicitor general and chief prosecutor of vile opportunism, making a political football out of something so old, and private, in the process, making an embarrassing spectacle of Albania. Still, it had to be followed.

So, he had been keeping up?

He had been watching, life being so constricted.

Constricted?

Naj made a bored face. He ran a disco.

They could understand. They had asked him to appear to testify about the general's relation to the statuette, and what he knew of Tile, personally, and of his pursuit. Had he known General Pollo for a long time?

Yes. He was a supporter of their club. He came to games. He'd visit the team—sometimes before, sometimes after—to offer his congratulations—sympathy—whatever. He had been a grand old gentleman, and was a true patriot.

After the general was incarcerated, he had stayed in touch?

He had.

He'd even visited the general in prison?

A couple of times.

Twelve times.

That sounded about right.

And he had visited him in hospital after his being attacked in his cell?

Yes. The general had asked to see him.

What did he want?

Sympathy, poor fellow.

What had they talked about?

Pretty much as always. The old days. How bad prison food was, and, about getting stabbed in the neck, how poor security was.

Did he say anything about his idea of using the statuette in negotiations for parole?

No. He had read about that. His guess was that the general thought of it when he saw the brouhaha over it, after the fiasco in Venice.

When he visited the general in the hospital that last time, he'd known that Pablon was after the statuette, and had hired Mr. Tile, hadn't he?

Yes.

Did the general know Mr. Tile was looking for it?

He had no idea.

He hadn't told the general?

No—why would he? Like he said, he didn't know then the general had the thingy, or that it had been in the institute.

The Marxist-Leninist Institute?

None other.

When had he learned that it was in the general's collection he had stored at the Marxist-Leninist Institute?"

State objected—facts not in evidence.

Sustained.

Very good. When had he first heard of the statuette?

When Tile first told him about it—after he met with Pablon.

Mr. Tile had told him about that meeting?

They were chatting. Tile dropped by. It came up, talking about what was new with him. They'd both thought it was funny—because of the ref angle.

Had Mr. Tile told him its subject matter?

He had.

Did he tell him what had happened when he tried to see Mrs. Skanderj-Pollo, then still Ms. Tajismini, at Gallery Harmoni about it?

He mentioned it.

Had he said how she had rebuffed him when he tried to talk to her about the statuette?

He'd said she sent the police to visit with him.

What had he thought? Had he believed him?

Sure. He'd had a laugh about it. He could imagine a lady feeling a bit uneasy if that hulk rolled up wanting to talk about art.

So—Pablon. Had he met Pablon himself?

He'd never actually met him.

Not even at the ill-fated game?

No.

What had he thought when he heard that Pablon was after the statuette?

What was there to think? It was weird. What else?

Was he interested in the statuette?

He was curious—like everybody else.

One last, jungle drums said he had alerted the Italians. Any truth in that?

He'd heard that too but it wasn't true.

On cross, State wondered—the referee from the worst game in the history of the franchise comes to town looking for a naughty statuette and gets in touch with a goalkeeper he once sent off and—if they remembered correctly—he and Mr. Tile thought it was funny?

They had.

When he learned that the general had the statuette and hoped to use it to negotiate parole had he thought that was funny too?

Pardon?

When had that been—that he learned the general had ideas about parole?

Like everybody else, in the news—when the general filed suit for ownership.

Not before?

No.

Had he been the least concerned?

Concerned? When? About what?

When the statuette became news. Had he been concerned about what it suggested, about what might come out about the old regime, the old state, in which he had place and stature?

Rubbish.

Had he ever heard the theory that the attempt on the general's life was precisely to keep the statuette out of play?

He didn't buy any of that.

Perhaps, but had he ever heard such a theory?

He'd heard it.

Given his—place—and—stature in the old state wouldn't he have preferred the statuette had never come into play?

The idea that such a thing would embarrass the "old state," or him? That was their bull. There was nothing and nobody left to embarrass. The old state had been swept away. Who cared? And now, where were they? The new state—fighting a businesswoman for possession of a commodity of dubious value, much less national interest. Why were they so eager to have it? What were they planning on doing with it if they won? Why were they hyping the situation? The thingy? Mrs. Skanderj-Pollo paid for it. Why not get out of the way and let her have it?

Did he have any idea how Mr. Tile had gotten wind of the statuette's actual whereabouts?

He had heard that Mr. Tile had a 'phone tip.

Had Mr. Tile told him that?

No. He'd heard it somewhere—he wasn't the only one who knew Tile was looking for it. People knew about it. There was talk.

And he'd gotten to hear about it.

Yes. People knew that he and Tile were friends.

So the whole affair was part of a conversation?

In some corners, yes, one could say that.

Among whom?

Check the web traffic.

And he was kept informed?

He shrugged.

Had he ever been to the archive?

No.

When had he learned that Mr. Tile had visited there and that he, and Ms. Tajismini and her friend, Mrs. Fagu, were on their way to Venice chasing after Pablon?

He heard what happened when everybody else did—when the news got back to town.

Tile hadn't told him anything?

About what?

About leaving for Venice.

No.

Then, had he been surprised?

By what?

By all of it—that the statuette had been in the archive, that Mr. Tile located it, that Pablon had it, and that Tile, Ms. Tajismini and Mrs. Faqu had been in pursuit.

Surprised? That the thingy was in the archive? No.

And that Mr. Tile knew to look there.

He had enough sense to take the tip seriously. The general was known to have an historic collection. It was a shame though, how poor security was there on the new state's watch. That Tile had chased off to Venice didn't surprise him.

Hm. Yes. Well. By the way—was he aware that there was no record of a request for police action, or of officers being dispatched in relation to a complaint of Ms. Tajismini or anyone else at or around the time in question?

No. That was the first he'd ever heard of that.

The jungle drums were silent on that score?

None he listened to ever said a mumbling word about anything like that.

They thanked him. That was all.

11

Leo was pleased. Jasmine was pleased. She thrilled at Naj reminding them that she had paid for the statuette.

In the evening she sat with Fatima at the kitchen table. Fatima had her cards. She smoked *kif.* Jasmine shuffled, reshuffled and shuffled again. Fatima spread the deck in a sweeping arc. Jasmine should pick three. She turned over the ten of diamonds, the two of clubs, and the jack of hearts.

Fatima tutted and rocked. She should pick three more.

Jasmine turned over the four of hearts, and the sevens of clubs and diamonds.

The archive guard was lying. She could see seven men—two groups, one of four, and one of three.

Should they recall him? He'd only lie again.

True. But hear how.

The guard was on furlough. Having no online capacity, he appeared from a neighbor's game-room decorated with pennants of Tile's and Naj's old club. The Court thanked him. Jasmine's lawyers thanked him. They wouldn't keep him. There were just one or two things that they hoped to clarify? He'd do his best to be of help. When Mr. Tile had come looking for the statuette—how had it been? How had what been? What sort of night was it? Regular—a regular night. What had he been doing? What he always did. And what was that? Making his rounds on the hour, like he always did—between times, keeping an eye on the security monitors. Monitors? In the booth, for the security cameras. Cameras? There were twelve—four covering the perimeters of the building, eight inside—one for every room. Were these cameras recorded? Normally, yes. Normally? Yes—Mr. Tile's visit wasn't recorded—looking into why not they'd found the problem—a malfunction at the interface owing to a faulty connection. So—a hardware rather than software problem. Yes. Any idea how long that had been going on? For four days at least before Mr. Tile visited, they thought, working backwards. So—from the second at least recordings of all of the cameras were affected? Yes—at least four days. How had he known it was Mr. Tile who wanted to get in? He rang the bell, he checked the backdoor monitor and saw him—the cameras were working, they just weren't recording. Ah—had he been on duty when Mr. Pablon and or his associates can reasonably be thought to have visited? Let him think—the third was his day off—he was back on the fourth—Mr. Tile came the sixth—he had no way of knowing when in there Pablon and his pals visited. Pity. The problem had been found and fixed—a loose wire. Jasmine's lawyers were delighted to hear that. State had no questions but declared for the record that they would open an investigation into who or what was responsible for the loose wire in the archive's surveillance system. The guard was thanked and excused.

Notwithstanding that it was alleged to have been a hardware rather than software malfunction, the cyber interface opened. Jasmine's lawyers moved to have State produce the logs and records of the archive, and of the Marxist-Leninist Institute. State were asked if latter such records existed, and did they have them? State replied that they did. They had the archive's records, and the institute's, but didn't have the product from the institute's. How was that? The archive's records were straightforward. But State analysts were finding anomalies in the institute's way of encrypting records that were making them difficult to crack. They asked for time and were granted a day to comply.

12

Jasmine's lawyers told her to be prepared to testify in case.

Fatima reluctantly read her cards again. When Jasmine turned over the two of clubs again—along with the aces of spades and clubs—she could only smile.

Jasmine frowned.

Came a knock.

"Darling?"

"Oo Lofti, Lofti."

"Hello, Darling—oh, hello, Fatima."

"Mister Leo."

"Getting ready for tomorrow?"

"I am trying."

"Good, darling, good. What think you, Fatima?"

"Allah be praised."

"Indeed indeed."

"Oo Lofti, I'm so sorry the family have to endure this on top of everything else—and you, my poor darling."

"Tut, tut, my love. We all understand. You are not responsible for things going the way they have."

"I never dreamed the government would care so much."

"Elections are coming. People want to score points."

"State are mean, trying to make me out a would-be thief. It isn't going to be easy to keep my temper."

"You'll be fine."

"Oh—Lofti Lofti—I—."

"Sh. Darling. Listen, go to bed. Get some sleep. No? Fatima, you tell her."

"What ever shall I wear tomorrow?"

"Whatever you wear—you're bound to be stunning!"

"What mask should I wear? Do I have to wear a mask?"

"Gosh—I don't know. Perhaps—at least until you have to speak? I don't know. It's best to play safe."

In the morning she dressed in black and went to the gallery—open by appointment only. She would appear from there. She hadn't made up her mind about wearing a mask, her mouth being one of her best features, and greatest communications assets. Still, she had one handy.

An hour before hearings were to convene, her lawyers rang excitedly. Records of the dates and terms of the general's storing his collections at the institute had been delivered—

they couldn't say how—and presented to the tribunal. State's case had collapsed. Formal notice of the ruling had been posted. Jasmine was free, keeping a social distance, to make an appointment to fetch the statuette from the archive.

Word spread fast. BigTime 7 TV News got in touch wanting to know, would she be willing for a reporter and camera crew to accompany her from a safe social distance when she went to collect the statuette, and perhaps be there when she took it from its box? From what they understood, they'd have to pixilate the image but it would be great television.

That sounded interesting. She would think it over.

13

Enver gazed out over the Pacific. Day was done. But for the plague he was sitting pretty. He'd leased the condo to a stock broker at a hefty rate the day after signing the paperwork with Jasmine and flown first-class to America to live high on the hog.

He'd watched the hearings, seen what happened after, and was finding it very difficult to live with the idea of waiting another minute to telephone Pablo. Bracing himself, he took a deep breath and pressed HOME.

"Hey, Siri—make a WhatsApp video-call to PP mobile, please—thank you."

"Making a WhatsApp video-call to PP mobile."

Purr-purr. Purr-purr. Purr—squeak.

"Harmoni? What is it? What time is it? Good God, you really shouldn't call at this hour. My sister—."

"Sorry, PP, I couldn't wait."

"You couldn't wait for what?"

"Another minute—obviously you have not heard the news."

"Obviously. Is there something new? Seems to me since forever as if it's all the same same same—faces in masks—it's terrifying. I gave up watching anything weeks ago."

"I can't believe you didn't follow proceedings in Tirana."

"I know the story."

"You wrote it! Permit me catching you up on the glory. There's been an exciting conclusion."

"Really? Wait, please, let me move. Hold on a minute."

He got up, put on his robe and slippers, and traversed his flat. The parquet squeaked.

"How is Los Angeles?"

"Paradise."

"Really? Where are you?"

"I have a charming bungalow in Venice."

"Hahaha—really?"

"On a canal."

"That's funny."

"It's sunset. The water has grown amazingly clear since the pandemic."

"In Venice too, one hears—dolphins have returned."

Reaching his study Pablon snapped on his desk lamp and sat. On the wall behind him hung an original Dürer "Melancholy," and on a table below stood the statuette.

"So, what is the news?"

"So—the news is: Jasmine won her case!"

"Not so loud."

"Sorry—it's just so funny. A TV crew filmed. Sami—in mask, face-shield and gloves..."

"Sami? He's funny. I'm glad to hear he's alive."

"I too! So, anyway—Sami goes into the archive and comes out with the box—cut to the gallery—he arrives, gets the box out of the car—my old Mercedes!—goes in, puts it on that big table in the back—the one by the window—it was great—so great. He proceeds to open it, undoes the wrapping and—*voilaaaa*—the dumbbell! And the coffee can full of cigar ashes!"

"*Diplomatico* ashes no less."

"Their faces!?! Pleeeease!"

"Those were expensive. We smoked and smoked. I can still smell them!"

"Viva Cuba! They were worth it. The fines too. Everything. Well worth it—three boxes?—tipping off the Venetian cops *avanti*—genius."

"Thank you."

"I'm delighted to have been part."

"You were integral, dear boy."

"The good Dr. and Mr. Vari will be calling to crow too before long, no doubt."

"No doubt."

"And Tile? You know—I feel for him, shall we say? In a way? Our discussion of iconography was great fun."

"Tile—poor Tile indeed—poor poor Tile. He was genuinely shocked when I showed him the red card. His eyes. He was perplexed so certain was he. He felt wronged. When he went mad? I tell you—the fear was exquisite. I could have come in my shorts."

"You're a *böse, böse mann*, *Señor* Pablo Pablon."

"God bless the Italians. I'm sure they x-rayed the box and understood immediately that somebody was fooling somebody. And your Jasmine?"

"She'll be wondering if the Italians didn't pull a fast one."

"Ha. It was us, dear Enver. We were the fast ones."

14

Jasmine needed a hot bath. Fatima drew one and added bubbles. Jasmine tiptoed in and relaxed in the tingle. Fatima poured her a glass of champagne.

It had been Enver all along.

She rang him.

"Jasmine?"

"Congratulations."

"Jasmine, darling. Thank you."

"You're welcome."

"Most gracious of you to ring."

"Where are you?"

"California."

"California. How are things in California?"

"Bug apart—great, thanks. Tirana?"

"Quiet."

"Lockdown?"

"Yes. There?"

"Partial. A frightening number go without masks—some militantly, some madly. Conflicting beliefs make this an interesting country."

They were silent.

"Anyway—I only wanted to say, 'congratulations'—congratulations. Stay safe."

"Thanks. I'll try. You too."

"I will—bye-bye."

She'd show the coffee tin, the ashes and dumbbell, with the box, on a pedestal—maybe a catafalque—the photograph on an easel—a wreath with a motto—good luck?—farewell?—(to be decided)—white lilies. Sad lighting—a fresh title—call it… (to be continued)…

15

Winnetou's was shut. So was damn everyplace. Tile crawled into bed and tried to read. It was no good. Quine's holism gave way quickly to a deep wish to be fucking Cyn. One good thing—Liverpool looked set to win the English Premier League championship after thirty years.

Across town, Cyn was in the sauna pouring cold water on the Scandinavian rocks and inhaling the steam. She ached. Emerging from the cedar chamber, she beat herself for some time with a eucalyptus whisk, picturing Spanish *Flagellistas*. Finally exhausted she clasped her hand over her clean-shaven mound and plunged into the immersion tub without hesitation, the next step in bathing her way to feeling clean. The icy cold took her breath away.

Instead of with her in the heat, Dr. Ali was in his studio, systematically stenciling waves of enlarged Covid-19 particles all over his National Museum Series canvasses. It felt active, coherent, satisfying, compositional, transcendent, projective, direct, fresh, a statement of fact, a summary, a glyph, a meme, primal. He could scream.

Purr-purr—purr-purr.

"Djmitri. What's op?"

Shikoni! [Look Out!], Ali Faqu, 2020, oil on canvas, 365.76 x 274.32 cm (12' x 9')

“An ancient style of painting.”

“Ho-ho-ho.”

“’smatter? You down?”

“Vacant.”

“Vacant?”

“You know—empty.”

“Sounds not good.”

“It ain’t.”

“Feeling you.”

“You painting?”

“No. The Seoul Sisters keep me busy. You?”

“Lucky you. I’m painting.”

“What?”

“Viruses. I’m putting them all over the Museum Series.”

“That’s sick, dude.”

“Sick?”

“You’re laying patterns of Covid-19 particles on top of your old negations?”

“Right.”

"That's sick decorative shit, dude. It's like Matisse goes to war or something—TV graphics."

"Pah! Have you been tested?"

"Bebe and Kiki have. I haven't been out since the virus hit. I wash my hands. I wear a mask. I keep my distance. I have everything delivered. I handle it with care. I dream of vaccine—anti-bodies."

"You really think the particle idea is bad?"

"Dude, it's stir craziness, as bad as Quinnychloroquine or whatever the hell it is."

◆ ◆ ◆

In love, with each other, and the idea of themselves, Bari and Dr. Nova moved in and began streaming living together.

The pixilation engineer at Big 7 TV News had her hands full, and, notwithstanding audio delay, audio had to be on their toes.

◆ ◆ ◆

Dr. Giorgio Giorgio and Mr. Tiki Vari had been in the kitchen of their shuttered restaurant in the south of France when they heard the news.

To stop gaps, Mr. Vari was working as an archivist at the Léger Museum in Biot. Dr. Giorgio was teaching English online to a young man sheltering on Cap d'Antibes in the villa of the son of the American film producer who had discovered Cliff

Robertson. He would be going to Hollywood when things got back to normal. Dr. Giorgio fantasized about being taken along.

"Let us drink to our happy ending."

"Hm—yum. What is this?"

"Italian—a *Montepulciano d'Abruzzo* for a change. Like it?"

"Very tasty. Cheers."

"Cheers."

"To our happy ending."

"And exquisite boredom."

"Are you really bored?"

"Hm—no, not really."

◆ ◆ ◆

Naj drove to visit his mother.

Ninety-one, she still lived on the family farm not far from the village where Jasmine was born, more interesting than ever, just north of Alexander the Great country, and Cleopatra country. What a couple they would have made.

Tinga-ling-ling-ling—tinga-ling—.

"Lofti? What's up? I was just thinking of you and Jasmine."

"Naj—just ringing to say, thank you again. Thank you from the family."

"Thank you, Leo, and your family. Regards and respects all 'round, please."

"I shall. Life is funny."

"How is Jasmine?"

"She's quiet."

"Really?"

"Yes. Like a volcano is quiet—between eruptions."

"Haha."

"She's already making plans."

"Good—good for her."

Upon arriving he parked in the inner court, put on his mask and gloves, dismounted and went to greet his mother, already waiting at the front door.

Her eyes glistened with joy above her mask. They kissed, mask to mask, went in and settled down to wait for a proper vaccine. The Russians claimed to have one—Sputnik V. He had been offered an injection but declined. Russians weren't to be trusted in things like that.

16

Tex enjoyed playing the greatest known predator of them all, stalking into the arena to his signature music—borrowed from *Cleopatra*—the Elizabeth Taylor version—the Ides of March scene—to which he had had added a slow T-Rex style jungle beat with lots of anal woof.

In the ring he was T-Rex—eyes beams, homed in, feeling almost as if UV light sensitive—enemies seeming to glow. He would bare his teeth and, roaring, spring on them, going for their throats, their ears. The cameras zoomed in. The crowd imitated his roar, baying for blood. The network loved him.

It was fun. Bari could be a wrestler. That'd be a trip. "The Leprechaun." And Perly—"Goliath and The Leprechaun"—that'd be a tag-team—though—? Poor Perly. In court over that queer art mess. Man o man. Not even wrestling could save him. He imagined Bari and Tile drinking in Winnetou's.

Perly reminded him in one way of Winnetou. Both were images of alienated dedication—Perly to his nature, without apparent reflection or qualm—Winnetou to his character, knowing full well. In that register, Perly was a bit of a sad story—a performative subject self. Winnetou was of course pure fiction—created a noble savage, working with the white man, ready even to die for his abstractions, on principle,

Hill Country Bluebonnet Landscape with Enchanted Rock, Porfirio Salinas

without expecting or caring even to be accepted as his equal, in that, his moral superior—perhaps, there, May's alter ego, rather than Old Shatterhand, his history.

As for the painting? He'd never forget it, but didn't think much of it. He'd listened to Perly countless nights go on about the opacity of gouache, the resulting flatness, how that affected the sense of space, how the silver worked, the illusions of depth, terrain etc., etc.—more than once to a chicken he would score with later, who liked the way the big man smooth talked art.

His Aunt Sophia had dragged him to an exhibition of Porfirio Salinas's bluebonnet paintings. Salinas was President Lyndon B. Johnson's favorite painter. He really caught them. The Winnetou didn't catch much. It was a genuine Djmitri, from his student days at the Art Academy. It almost worked. If you knew where you were, you knew the figure was meant to be Winnetou—*basta*. If you knew the books, ditto. If you were familiar with the films, ditto again, but likeness problems came into it, complicating what you could say about the scene or the figure. You'd know the painting copied a pose at a moment from the film, and that you were meant to be seeing Pierre Brice playing the role, standing by the Silver Lake with his horse Iltschi. But you'd also see that the pose wasn't quite right, that the scenery was a bit off, and that the figure didn't look like Brice. If you knew Brice but didn't know that he'd played the role, the figure would fail to signify beyond the basic relation. If you weren't totally smashed, knew nothing about the books or films and had never heard of Winnetou, but knew a little about American history you would see at least what the figure was meant to be from the color of his skin, his outfit, and his horse's blanket. If you didn't know the books or films, the question, what he was, remained. Race and ethnicity came into it in a serious way. Two Americans once almost came to blows over what it was proper to call him. One insisted on "Indian," the other, "Native American." Tex had been able to put an end to it before anybody got hurt by pointing out that Winnetou's Apache.

He passed on trying to imagine why Bari had quit. The rumor he was a cop was absurd. He doubted winter was to blame. Whatever it was—bless him. The boy was a great emcee—pulling faces, putting on airs, speaking in voices, reading people right—streetwise. For sure the club was a dead end for him as an actor of course. Without him, it felt empty. When the virus hit, he'd had to shut it down. Some days it felt like that might be the end.

He didn't watch TV, so had yet to see Bari do the weather, and couldn't bring himself to ring. Mrs. Skanderj-Pollo v Albania he followed piecemeal on WhoToob and found most of it a bit dull, some even pathetic, until Naj. Naj was ominous. It was easy to believe the old rumor that he had been a secret policeman. He could imagine for instance his knowing that General Pollo had the statuette stashed and was thinking of trading it for freedom. He could have wanted to help… or, to kill the idea… either way, how better to force the situation one way or the other than get Pablon in to work Perly? The old boy

Winnetou dhe Iltschi [Winnetou and Iltschi], Djmitri Djmitri, 1987, gouache on canvas, 91.44 x 121.92 cm (3' x 4')

had plenty football connections. But, hell, what did he know? He didn't know.

Contemplating the possibilities made him hungry. He warmed some Wolf Brand chili, and Ranch Style beans—canned delicacies still sent him by his dear Auntie—and dialed up NexFux_orgy.net.

◆ ◆ ◆

WARNING!—as last we shall see him Tex is about to make up his mind which of two pornographic films to watch. In what follows explicit references to certain sex acts, and some vulgar colloquialisms will be in play. Please decide here whether or not to continue reading.

◆ ◆ ◆

Tex likes good old fashioned storylines. Tonight it's a toss up between *Julius' Seizure* and *One Step Forward, Two Steps Back*.

He likes *Julius' Seizure* mainly for two scenes—one where lean and hungry Cassius works hard on proud Brutus to win him over to the idea of offing Caesar, and one where Calpurnia works hard on Julius trying to keep him home from the office on the Ides. Apart from her hollering "giddyap" during the title event, the dialog came from Shakespeare and really Zenned things up.

He plumps for *One Step Forward, Two Steps Back*.

The sense of meaningful narrative aspect came from the world of Andy Warhol in the 'eighties. Bits played at "The Rectory," most at "Studio 45," a celebrity disco where "Randy Paxhall" often went nights, looking for Mr. Right, arriving in a big black ZIL-115, with entourage—a dandy called "Red Blues," an androgynous creature called "Mandy Dear," an older beauty called "Polly," and "Jimo," a geeky type in horn-rim glasses—no doubt Robert "Bob" Colacello, from whose book—*Holy Terror*—a great deal of the shape of things had been lifted. Bari played the doorman. Whenever "Randy" went in or out of the joint he would make eyes at Bari and manage somehow to rub his crotch in passing. Favorite scenes included a split-screen where "Randy" and "Imolda Darkos" talk shoes while she dances barefoot under the table on "Red's" junk. There was a sweet lesbian scene in the Ladies, where "Blanca," a pretty woman with a big mouth and eyes, worries to "Polly" that her husband "Dick" is having an affair with a horse while she and "Polly" lick and rub one another. Tops was in a private room where "Randy" whines to "Jimo" that he hasn't had anything "up there" in "aaaaages" while shooting Polaroids of "Erector Fewgo" giving Bari a blowjob. It turns out that "Randy" has been approached by the FBI who want him to share his photos and tapes of his meetings with his political clients—the "Shah," "Imolda," "Fancy Raygun," "Senator Armpits" and his wife, "Harriet," and a few others. In a flashback, "Randy" tells "Red" that he's disappointed how corrupt everything seems to be getting, and that he "reaaaally" doesn't like the idea. "Red" advises him to go ahead. He can pick and choose what he wants them to see, and make them pay through the nose. "Randy" whines he guesses that might be fun, but begs

"Red" to make the deal. "Red" agrees and meets with a female agent in her office. They negotiate "Randy's" payoff during anal sex. As he withdraws to splash come on her ass, he promises her a "Lenin" screen print.

Dramatic tension came from the burning question, would "Randy" eventually meet Mr. Right, find love, and get something up his ass. It never came of course.

Tex loves "Randy" for speaking truth to life, love, and power. The title payoff came from "Jimo" telling "Randy" that, even if he found Mr. Right, standing ready and right behind him, he wouldn't know what to do—take one step forward, or two steps back.

THE END

PICTURE CREDITS

Cover
Court Summons
Unknown

Page 32
Dizmuzwiz Show Poster
Unknown

Page 102 & 106
Playing Cards
Unknown

Page 118
Shikoni!
Ali Faqu, 2020
Image courtesy of the artist

Page 124
Hill Country Bluebonnet Landscape with Enchanted Rock
Porfirio Salinas, 1959
Image Courtesy of Foltz Fine Art,
Houston, Texas

Page 127
Winnetou dhe Iltschi
Djmitri Djmitri, 1987
Image courtesy of the artist

After Math
has been printed in a limited edition
of 600 hardcover copies.

The book has been designed in the United States — in Chicago, Illinois, and Los Angeles, California — by author Mayo Thompson, graphic designer Dan Osborn, and record conglomerate Drag City (Incorporated).

It has been printed on 45# Alternative Natural Offset paper from Resolute Forest Products of Montréal, Quebec, Canada, with printing and binding capably handled in April of 2022 by Bang Printing of Brainerd, Minnesota.

The text of this book has been set in Garamond Premier Pro, designed by Robert Slimbach and released in 2005 by Adobe Systems Incorporated of San Jose, California. The roman characters are based on Claude Garamond's original hand-cut masters from the mid-1500s, while the italic characters, as is common with Garamond type, are based on an italic type by Garamond's contemporary, Robert Granjon.

Chapter titles are set in Helvetica Neue, produced by Linotype-Hell AG, now known as Monotype GmbH, located in Bad Homburg, Germany. It is a reworking of Helvetica, which was introduced in 1957 by Max Miedinger and Eduard Hoffmann of the Haas Type Foundry in Münchenstein, Switzerland.